W9-ACQ-834

UNTIL THE NEXT ENCHANTMENT

The man who tells his own story in this novel is leading a double life of a quite new kind. To others he is someone to be envied, perhaps even respected: the roving correspondent for an influential Milanese weekly, who travels freely about Europe, beyond the Iron Curtain and to Africa, interviewing the leaders of nations: a commentator who is listened to. To him none of this matters any more, now that the post-war opportunity for the political renovation of his Italy—the revolution that never was—has been passed by.

The centre of his life has become his tormented passion for Joan and the 'enchantments' that she holds—'her unrivalled capacity for distilling moments of love as though they were drops of the rarest essence'. Into his daydreams about their relationship flow memories of his childhood, fantasies about Joan's enigmatic past, and visions of episodes from Milan's chequered history. But the intense, fevered world of his imagination is threatened more and more, right up to the climax, by the cutting edge of daylight.

Also by Carlo Castellaneta

VILLA DI DELIZIA

UNTIL THE NEXT ENCHANTMENT

By

Carlo Castellaneta

Translated by
GEORGE KAY

1970

CHATTO & WINDUS
LONDON

Published by
Chatto & Windus Ltd
40 William IV Street
London W.C.2

*

Clarke, Irwin & Co. Ltd
Toronto

SBN 7011 1576 9

© Rizzoli Editore, Milan 1968

Translation © Chatto & Windus Ltd. 1970

All rights reserved. No part of this
publication may be reproduced, stored
in a retrieval system, or transmitted, in
any form, or by any means, electronic,
mechanical, photocopying, recording or
otherwise, without the prior permission
of Chatto & Windus Ltd.

Printed in Great Britain by
Northumberland Press Ltd.,
Gateshead

CONTENTS

PART ONE

'There's a mistake writers make,' Joan went on. She settled the pillow more comfortably at her back. 'They believe that anything that happens to them is important. Even their illnesses.'

The rain kept on falling. Now the landscape of fir-trees had vanished from the window, as mist invaded the whole valley.

'You call them novels?' she added, still considering her book. 'This pack of little betrayals, tears and regrets, each one of them pretending to be a French Revolution!'

'But the style matters,' I said. 'Doesn't the way a book is written affect you?'

She picked up the telephone and ordered something to drink. At the little half-opened windows the damp woodland was edging in, the cool of the sheets was so pleasant, the room lined with fir.

'Iced,' Joan repeated.

Drinking champagne in bed was her only weakness. She stretched out again, took up her book with an expression which showed that she was prepared for the worst. Now the rain beat in light gusts. She concentrated on her reading, the waiter brought in the ice-bucket on a tray.

'How many pages?' she asked.

'Sixty. What about you?'

'Eighty-one.'

She squinted at my page.

9

'Liar. Fifty-eight.'

'All right,' I agreed. 'Fifty-eight.'

We read, we dipped our lips in the wide glasses, it rained in bursts.

'D'you think it'll rain on Mount Stella?'

I nodded, but did not abandon my book. Hers had ended up on the bedside rug again. We kissed briefly, then, observing the ritual, dipped our lips in the champagne once more, a longer kiss followed, with champagne running from the tilting glasses on to the bedspread.

'That's enough now. I'll leave you to read.'

She curled up beside me. The shade cast by the June thunderstorm had darkened the colours of the room's timbered parts. I turned on the bedside lamp, and my gaze was caught by the spot of warm light that played on her hair as she lay beside the chapter on sabotage: because the correct procedure is to open other fronts, not reinforce those that are already holding against the enemy.

'Joan,' I cautioned.

Without any obvious intention she was fondling me, gentle and tormenting.

'Stop it, it's hardly the . . .'

It seemed terribly out of place too, just at the moment when the balance was turning against guerrilla action, our forces being scattered in patrols over too wide an area.

'Please—it's not just a game.'

'But it is.'

'It's what gives you babies.'

I tried to gain ground: towards the Sierra, towards the first spurs of the Andes, right at the end of the chapter. I tried to underline principles which I myself guessed were fundamental in a certain kind of struggle, such as the need for taking military action before attempting political propaganda, and then we shouldn't be tiring ourselves too much when we had agreed to tackle the peak the following morning, if it was fair, armed with crampons and axes.

I closed the book again, with my forefinger still on guard at my place.

'What now?' I sighed.

There was a rumble of thunder, going right down our bodies, it seemed to me, announcing a storm. I was grateful to her for the look she wore then of being won, not winning.

'What now, hell-cat?'

The ridge of the Lepontines, the guides will tell you, reaches nearly ten thousand feet up. Many of its peaks, in fact, rise higher. Pizzo Stella is one of these, a pyramid of solid diorite, which I had not chosen at random from among the two hundred and sixteen glacial mountains of Lombardy, but because of its south-east face where a broad mass of rock-debris leads safely to the summit.

We had begun climbing at dawn and now, with the Chiavenna hut beneath us, saw that the snow which had fallen in the night cloaked the main glacier deposit itself, covered the little serac which I remembered, a little way to one side, and similarly the ice of the glacier-tongue, greenish and glassy, was dusted over white as well.

'A partisan?' Joan asked.

I was strapping on her crampons for her.

'Yes,' I said. 'Just here. With a bullet hole in his temple.'

The sun began to touch the peak, the cold was really biting.

'D'you think I'll make it?'

Her eyes just showed from the encircling wool of her balaclava, she seemed happy, said yes, she was, and I attacked the steep with short, quick blows of the ice-axe, as I had seen them doing twenty-five years earlier when I first went up that very stretch as a boy.

'Is it all like this?'

'Only the first bit. Then we can take off the crampons.'

The satisfaction of seeing her, Joan, climbing behind me, and the great silence broken only by the steel point's cutting into the ice, and then the light rattle of the ice chips down the slope, the giddiness that came when I looked down each time to see the fragments slide valley-wards, streaking the snow as they went, and her tied to me, bringing the knot at her waist round towards the mountain, when we doubled back on the diagonal, five metres of red nylon between us, and I almost wished she would miss her footing and plunge, so that she could see how well I took the strain.

'How goes it?'

'Fine.'

'We're there. Don't weaken.'

Fifteen hundred feet above us the snow was now shining in the first dazzling sunlight, I went on trampling the fresh layer and cutting out foot-holds in the ice beneath, solid as ever; worked on with a burning well-being in my body, with renewed desire, the taste for struggle—that silence and the dull hacking of the ice-axe, the natural state of the hunt, of risk, raising glittering sparks. This must be what makes man give a damn when (angel of the snows or the deep sea) he seems about to launch out all alone: the gratification in striving for others, a family from which all civilised living springs, an institution created specifically to tame the man of the Fourth Warm Interval, and quite apart from any Rousseau myth, we had reached the edge of the central depression.

I helped her again to take off the crampons.

'Now we're making for the top, a couple of hours and we're there.'

'Is that it you see?'

'No, that's the false top.'

'A couple of hours?'

I had known for a good time how it would be. The peak was going to be like Joan herself, restless to the last to be overcome, but it seemed out of place to talk of love with this blue air outlining the summits.

I put down our haversack and we sucked lumps of sugar. Joan looked askance now at the walls of black limestone faintly powdered white, at the pyramid which loomed over us, menacing.

'This Mount Stella of yours,' she panted.

Celebrated by Bertacchi, the local poet. Never heard of him, she says. I had the pack on my back again, and the crampons hung there tinkled merrily.

'You see, this is the glacier of ablation and the one above is the glacier of formation . . . Think you'll make it?'

'I'll try. Have you done all the hacking?'

She displayed the icicles on her boots, the damp patches on her trousers, and fell in behind me again, taking more care because we had left the ice-pack now, and the boulders of the last slopes were easily dislodged. We went on in the blazing sun, stopped to smear our faces with cream, for the last height of all we freed ourselves of our windbreakers.

Twenty-five years ago, I thought. I was really pleased that I could manage it still, and above all that there were places that time did not score, except for the imperceptible creeping of the ice-cap, and the partisan that the soldiers brought down to the village with the black hole above his eye, climbing with Joan in that burst of light, the light of being alive, dazzled by the fulness as I would be by a memorable page, by a truth glimpsed, perhaps not more than a glimmer but compelling, a fulness you cannot hold, like a drug or a merry drunkenness, and then you contain the whole creation, lightly overcoming the scree, sidling between edges of rock, your weaknesses themselves take on a sense in the ultimate design, that, deceptive though it is, still shows in its twists and turns.

'How goes it?' Joan called from a few yards lower down.

'We're there, this is the peak we're on now.'

Fringes of white cloud had begun to fall upon the spread arc of the summits. Unbelieving, we looked back over our path, the blot of the firs down there, five hours trudge away, the terraced pastureland and the snow-field, gazing with the unconcern of the dear departed.

'What are you thinking?' she asked.

'Nothing: a little thrust from the heel, and we'd go straight up to heaven.'

'That's true. It's a pity not to believe in heaven.'

In passing the haversack to me, she knocked against a stone which broke from the slope and at once gathered speed, carrying a little avalanche with it, hurtling down until it disappeared, a moment's silence followed, then the thud, on a spur of rock, and I thought supposing we'd been there to stop it, I can imagine the three-column spread a brother reporter would have given us.

'Easy now: don't look back until we're up on top.'

It took us a good half hour to get there, breath coming short, and short of temper, too; radiant-faced.

'You've done it, Joan.'

She panted, swallowed with difficulty, and we embraced as if we had been first to make the direct ascent (in winter, too), in the wind that sets you swaying, and we sought shelter in a cleft, sinking knee-deep in the snow.

Now the view frightened us, with the sheer walls of the gully right below us, the eye of blue enamel that was Lago Angeloga, and across from us, the white and cobalt ridges of the Engadina, other peaks that I began listing for her, recognising each with excitement, and to the south the plain of Samolaco, as if caught in binoculars, detached.

We melted a handful of snow over our little stove and made hot soup, and were troubled at the thought of emptying the left-overs on the untouched white.

'I was just wondering,' I said, 'if I could make love up here supposing I wanted to. I don't think I could.'

'Why not?'

'I don't know, it would be like dirtying the view.'

'That's not it. You'd hold back because you were in the sight of God.'

'Don't joke, I'm talking seriously.'

'Of course you are: you see love as something dirty. Remember that discussion we had on that island of nudists?'

'I know. I should learn.'

'You'll never learn. You're an old moralist at heart.'

We had to put on our gloves and windbreakers again, and Joan her balaclava too. I couldn't recognise her as she licked the rims of the cans, only the highest peaks watched us eating, swaddled in all that padding, in a relentless wind.

'How high did you say it was?'

'Twelve hundred.'

'Why did it have to be just the Stella?'

'I don't know, perhaps because I climbed it as a boy.'

'You're forever searching for your childhood—that's it, isn't it?'

We ate chocolate. I told myself I would bring my daughter up here when she was big.

'But we're going to rest for the next few days.'

'Of course, darling. We're on holiday.'

'Where do you think they'll send you on your next assignment?'

'Why?'

'I'd like to come along with you once, say, to Africa.'

Our descent was slow, and dangerous too, as the ice layer had melted and the boulders slipped if you touched them, but I was glad she could count on me, on my knowing the mountain. Letting her go down first, I took the strain. At the snow-field we sat down together on my jacket, holding tight, and slid down the whole of the last slope to the bottom.

'That's what I like about you: you're still a boy.'

I wanted to tell her that she had made me a present of a wonderful day, and now we were leaping rhododendron bushes, carried down by our heavy boots, I falling and rolling with her in beds that always varied, the dried-up course of a river, round stones, the humped blankets in little private hotels, drinking deep of Joan, any danger of ground crumbling on the eastern slope being out of the question, we watched the dawn bloom between loosened shutter-bars, floating, coming up on top again, in the shipwreck of bedclothes, sometimes like today, not telling our fulness.

'Do you know this girl's just dead beat?'

At the lake we rested in the shelter, baked by sun, thirsting. We pulled off our boots and ran to dip our feet in the chilly water. At sunset we were back in the hotel, exhausted. A telegram was awaiting me that had arrived that morning.

'Joan,' I announced. 'Our holiday . . .'

I saw as if on a relief map the snow-fields, the cirques of the Alps, right under the ribs of the huge wing and the rivets that sent out flashes, twenty-five thousand feet up, and I did not try to recognise single peaks, barely allowing myself to be blinded by so much white, sunk back in the easy seat, and I wondered how many pairs of air-hostess legs, all alike, I could have counted from Tokyo to I don't know where, while I tried to imagine Joan in that quartermistress uniform.

17

She had insisted on taking me to the airport in her car. She had struck me as incredibly beautiful, with her snow sun-tan which the white two-piece set off, and which nonetheless I had forgotten as we landed at Zürich, where I was to take another plane on to Frankfurt, and thence to Dakar, my destination.

At Frankfurt it was raining, so the rain washed out even the footprints which with Joan I had left on Mont Blanc a few minutes earlier, and yet the bar of the air terminal was crowded, the scent of German sausage until the loudspeaker called and the expelled and the banned rose up, the brothers Robespierre among them, to board the tumbril which was an enormous Boeing made expressly to get across oceans.

I began to feel better, with the rainwater streaking the portholes, in the grey froth of cloud and the lowering time of day, beginning, as well, to make notes for my interview. Then, in the subdued chatter of a typical flight, I outlined a possible perfect life, going from plane to plane without break, say, a whole existence given up to action as the only possibility that might save you from the friction of days—second half of the revolution that never was—until I noticed how largely Joan came into it all, even the silliest diversion like this.

In my notebook I had written: (1) Do you think they will hang him? (2) What is your country's attitude to this prospect? (3) Do you consider that it will serve the African cause, if he is condemned?

For my part I would gladly have seen him hung from a gallows in the main square of Leo that they now call Kinshasa, and even imagined what reply the President would give. It was dinner time, a voice announced that we were flying over the Atlantic. On

18

board there were no fellow journalists. I dined, then loosened my tie and got ready to sleep: Joan stood on the terrace at the airport, waving her handkerchief, sequence from an old film, as rugs were handed out, and the lights switched on for those rocked by the burr of motors inside a pressurised aquarium.

I had never thought of taking my daughter there. You could tell her that we'll live on plankton, one day, and the depths of the sea will have no secrets. Instead your eyes went to the tench, every time that she turned to you, studying her features, because of the resemblance that took your breath away, yes, to Aldina, the first time she let herself be examined, seeing that I had discovered (in my father's night-time po) and consulted, too, one of those manuals on wedded hygiene that used to take the place of erotic books. Certainly it is not the best place, an aquarium, when your body is full of these urges, if the sea-turtle is gliding silently through his fresh-water tank, specially if the carassius auratus which turns out to be the goldfish landed at the stalls one carnival evening, you hear the ping-pong ball striking about the mouths of the glass bowls banteringly, Aldina who shrieks each time and her laugh gurgles right down you know where; specially if Joan is not going to stop twisting about like the velvet eel, savage and sinuous, and it would be wiser to make her stop, to change glass-panel, to put, in place of these images of the flesh, that of the Nile crocodile, with his glassy eye that, for a moment, stops the course of history.

So you stand: watching the shoals as they break up

and reform in new formations, all perfect, an aimless wandering without hope, suddenly the anostomus from South America flashes out, and you fool yourself into believing for a moment that something is about to happen, that not everything has been decided, you wait for a sign, an answer from these wraiths that gleam like enamel, and while you observe, quite coldly, the barely perceptible heaving of the gills, your instinct suffers the last attacks exactly at the point where the minute heating-plant reproduces the warmth of Sumatran waters, at an hour of day when you should be at work like everyone else: instead you have wandered away from that, are already lost in the little world of glittering scales, of the mysterious silence of the depths around Borneo, in the cathedrals of light where Joan rests unreachably, she is the garish simfysodon discus, that flower of the Amazon basin forced to rub against the pebbles of the River Ticino, we who were born for high deeds, and it is still her in the suckers of the octopus who stretches and draws in lovely arms, and then Aldina again, Aldina as a girl when she uncloses the pincers on the edge of her lair: there is nothing else, admit it, nothing else, seeing that here too you will fail to touch the greatness that you hunger for, better to go down gasping, inhaling the required amount of micro-organisms, be content to live in the illustrated tables of Linnaeus, put off to a better time the taste for resistance, glad to survive till tomorrow.

'Monsieur,' a voice called, bending over me. 'Monsieur. We are at Dakar.'

*   *   *

I was sure of it the moment I put my head out of the

plane door, from the shock of meeting that warm and fetid air that seemed to smell of burnt canes, welcome, in any case, at that moment, the eternal African stench, and reassured, too, by the red and green lights of the runways vanishing into the night mist. I went through the customs and got into a taxi. My seat was taken by a kind of lizard that flew off through the window, it's nothing, I told Joan, I explained to her that it is the fish they put into the ground, so that it can rot and become fertiliser, that is poisoning the air like this, because the tropical sun in this season dries excrement right up the moment you lay it on the ground, the sweat ran down the driver's neck quietly, and the Peugeot flew along at ninety towards the city.

Place de l'Indépendance, where the only reasonable hotel is to be found, was almost beautiful, deserted at four in the morning. I woke the doorman as he lay on a mat spread on the pavement, but I refused an air-conditioned room because a month earlier at Lagos the little cooling mechanism had kept me awake all night.

I wound up my alarm. Monsieur le Président would see me at ten, I had five good hours of sleep before me, were it not for the unbearable sultriness and the impossibility of quenching my thirst with a bottle of mineral water. I had put on the light in the bathroom, but could not decide whether to drink the water from those taps or not, I worried them, old taps of brass, and insects smeared out on the walls, displaying the marvels of Africa to Joan, opening my brief-case and taking out the toothpaste, but already far-away, through one of those wonders worked by memory that give the past back to us intact.

*　　　*　　　*

21

And so my father pointed out the window in the building, on the first floor, just level with the tram wires (the tram that passed there was the '29'), now you know how it was, that Sunday in May, he wore two elastic bands round his shirt-sleeves which were too full, there was a lot of dust on the leaves in the avenue, and my mother found herself lying back on the sofa before she had even said yes. A story just like any other that you would have had, only it was a Sunday in 1929, and he, who still called it Saint Petersburg, who made mistakes with English names, he made no mistake about rummaging inside her corset, her cloche-hat rolled over the floor, and there was that dust on the leaves in the avenue and in his bachelor room too, on the brass taps of the wash-basin, a room furnished largely with his case in which he kept, carefully folded, his diploma, the black and white shoes beside the pipe from the wash-basin, a half-empty tram went by shattering the Sunday quiet.

At last my mother opened her eyes, the pupils of them, blue, she being a Lombard-Venetian, unaware of the Saracen seed which mounted her womb. She said something; which my father did not catch, because she held him very tight in her arms.

Because of this, your restlessness is of old date, descended from that afternoon in May, Italy ended at the gates of Rome for them, neither had ever been to the seaside, and people could believe in the snapshots taken on the steps of the Cathedral, a pigeon balanced on their hand, content with life as they sat on a bench in the park, my mother with her hair cut gamine style in the act of climbing up the trunk of a chestnut tree, and he must have been thinking, just then, as he leant back on the balustrade at Montemerlo, of how he could have her in that girlish dress.

Now you know that this was on the Sunday before she came to the room my father rented in Viale Piave. Right through the winter he had bombarded her with letters, with short notes slipped between the pages of a book of verse, with roses which he bought one at a time from the flower girl opposite the Church of Suffrage, even an Alsatian came into it borrowed from who knows whom, and they posed with it for a photograph, don't be trusting, her mother would say, O girl, don't make a fool of yourself, and she was already cut out for that glittering Arab smile and those masterful ways: so she ended by giving in to him, overcome, as you in turn were to overcome other girls at the marrying age, employed in offices or in the big stores (the age of dressmakers being past), without ever asking yourself if they would suffer, after so much talk, the exact same phrases that he, in stripping her, must have whispered.

Not this one: Look—that other window, above the chemist's.

Then you both rose up. It was getting dark, because hours had flown, and the twilight played on the few things in the room, on that enamelled wash-basin, the bottle of aniseed, two half-filled glasses, the razor on the shelf above the wash-basin, the razor of a man from the South, complete with strop, a brimming ash-tray, the shaving brush streaked with dried soap.

Arms about one another, you went over to the window. My mother, unspeaking, in the presentiment that she had gambled her life. She listened to him as he talked on grandly: about new jobs, money, trips

23

they would take, cheap day-tours, right up to Venice, say. She could not tell then that it was going to take years before they stepped off the steamer at Piazza San Marco, and then steamer again to the Lido, carrying their lunch in a bag. She listened to him, enthralled and a little frightened too, by these possibilities that were outside her dressmaking universe, with a great longing to have a good cry; the people of Monforte came out of the Esperia cinema, the stall for ices, the tram trolleys hissing by, until she was pressed right back again on the sofa.

From the President's secretariat a woman answered in perfect French. His Excellency would receive me at ten o'clock exactly. On our paper they were very skilful at arranging these special articles, the absolute minimum of time and, so, minimum cost, and Joan would not be long without me.

It is cafés like this one that I choose by preference, with all their colonial rhetoric, the huge-bladed fan, the rickety straw chairs set out in a row, the coloured awnings, the filth at the foot of the bar, and the unfailing little heaps of sawdust on the floor, the hawkers' voices always the same, as they cry their wares, stubbornly offering you ivory pieces and ebony masks that are carved to one design from Magreb to the Atlantic Coast.

The taxi set me down at the palace entrance right in front of the sentry who was black and proud of his uniform. An usher in shorts, a medal on his breast, announced me to the President. I was shown in, I waited for a few moments in the odour of Dutch tobacco. His Excellency was hid by a magnificent basket of flowers, he waved graciously towards an easy chair in front of his Louis Quinze desk, and I at once drew out my notebook.

He answered calmly, clearing away imaginary particles with the back of his coal-black hand, slowly sucking on his pipe from behind gold-rimmed lenses, and I wondered what the weather would be like at Milan, realising with terror how much Joan counted in the possibilities which he, a head of state, a writer, was listing in answer to my question about the course Black Self-consciousness would take.

'And as a poet,' I said, 'what do you think of this business?'

He was greatly at his ease, and adamant, too, on the divide between politics and culture, which still troubled a lot of us in Europe, until he rose up to bring our conversation to an end. The interview had lasted less than half an hour, I had to get four or five typescript pages from it, and the President would read the outcome in our next number, the following week.

He invited me to join his entourage and come along to Saint-Louis, where they were opening a new school. I knew the town, at the mouth of the great river. I had been there once on the way from Mauritania, to dine with a French arms dealer. To have gone there now would have added a pendant to my article, but I wanted to get back home with the night flight and give Joan a surprise.

I lunched in a restaurant in the centre of town, tormented by shoe-shine boys who had made my life hell during those months at Algiers.

At the hotel I began writing my piece. Stripped to the waist, I struck the portable's keys as sweat ran from neck to haunch. I told Joan about it in a letter I posted before going out again. At sunset I called a taxi and had myself conveyed to Ngor, on the coast, half an hour's drive from Dakar. We had left Medina behind us, navigated at walking pace the crowds of poor devils, the eternal shanty-towns, the minarets fitted with loud speakers. There is a large hotel where the Americans come to spend week-ends, right on the sea, with an open-air swimming-pool and bar, all under the palms.

It was the book that, sooner or later, I would write about Africa which was the hope of all of us, which has been betrayed, flourishing with peanuts and mara-bouts, a tragic ballet of sweat, of tom-toms, of glitter-ing uniforms, so much truer in its witch-doctors and warriors with spears, with its wounds gaping rawly in the enamelled basins outside the shacks, in the roaring of bulldozers, this circus that has been born dead, of poor broken-down actors, with bare electric light-bulbs swinging in the open, in the villages, all the rejected merchandise of Europe dumped like refuse on these shores, as I ordered a whisky, Yvette nodded to me from a table where she sat with a pilot from the same airline.

The sun was a ball of fire in the ocean, that was as calm as the ocean can be at sunset, with the naked bodies of young negroes chasing one another along the shoreline. It was rather depressing to think of revolu-tion on this terrace for Americans, before Africa's soli-tude and mine, going over the lists of dead and wounded. I had barely looked at the paper when

Yvette joined me, thinner, I thought, since our affair in Nairobi.

We dined together, but she did not want to come up to my room.

'I'm getting married in a month's time.'

'Oh,' I said. 'Is he a pilot?'

She said he was a good boy, a business man from Lyons, and she gave me a look that begged for approval.

'Do you remember Nairobi?'

She said she did, but that we were not to think of it.

At two I was back at Yoff, the plane was taking on the last of its fuel. I fell dead asleep as soon as I had fastened my belt, and I woke at Frankfurt the next morning. In the afternoon I was in Milan which was beautifully hot to me.

I thought of dropping by at Joan's shop, all in all I was glad I had been faithful to her, but the surprise in store was for me.

'Madam's not here,' said the shop-girl. 'She's left town.'

'Left town?'

'Yes. She's gone to Paris, I think.'

It is probably because of this, you used to tell yourself: because of the daily fear that everything has already been decided. A fear with no greatness in it, bloodless, shameful, when all is told; that you will not know how to get out of it, that you will end by accepting the part you have been given. You know you will have to work really hard, with little hope of changing any-

27

thing, and the fear is also of letting things go some day and of simply getting by like Them. After all, others, better than you, better equipped, have ended up doing just that. The fear is of letting yourself be aware, each time you wait for Joan, and go to the door, and listen for the lift, the fear is that now you are alive no other way.

'Sorry,' she will say lightly. 'Am I late?'

Our fingers entwined on the white of bed linen, a little later.

You think of the sheet on which she lay, naked, like a chart, a star map. There is nothing else at all, you said, brushing her with your lips. You heard, away in the distance, the sounding horns of another planet. Your fear of not being alive had been tricked: suddenly a shiver of sweat gone cold, she stretches out her long legs between Peking and Hanio, pushing up on her elbows she raises her breasts, the most secret part of her body lies in the epicentre of guerrilla activity, it has taken several years to recognise, this cut of jungle at the burning frontier, the eternal Iron Triangle, a heat that almost equals the flames from naplam rockets: here is hell, the rice fields blackened, women and children like sticks, the charm of her arms when she stretches back her arm-pit and whispers, eyes closed: 'Did you like that?'

'A cat,' I shall say. 'That's what you are.'

But when, in what precise moment did all that begin? I know you were walking: *du côté de chez Swann*, if I am not wrong, skirting the enemy's bastions, the high gates within which a chauffeur, the great shining windows, the fittings of Swedish steel, perhaps a fountain with goldfish, but an invisible one, seen only in a jet of water amid the trunks of young plane-trees, and the plane-trees cross the terraces, and you were walking, eager to turn these buildings into a state home for the poor.

As you might know: on one of these floors, I believe the top one, Joan as a child trilled her 'Little Mountaineer' on a Steinway. The man in the apron who sprinkled water from a long spout, turned his head to watch me. The chauffeur paused a moment in wiping the limousine with a cloth, there was a sort of driveway of pure white gravel, perhaps you imagined how the little stones would spurt from under the tyres of a car that was taking you into the depths of the fortress.

A fairy story, for you who went to work in cast-off suède shoes, a gift from Uncle Peter, and, after, work, along to night classes in French; or, more likely, to indulge the first weakness that cracked your fury. Now you wonder what would have become of you, if you had been born as one of them, growing up among enormous teddy bears, scolded in German, and, like her, bred to the point of abuse.

'Nurse, I want to try your shoes on now.'

No. Yours was a different story, although it began not far from her elect quarter: the boarding-house in Viale Piave, the typical, average room in that block without a lift where you were conceived.

'What the devil were you doing in Paris, tell me?'

She got up to look for an ashtray, draping herself in a sheet as actresses in films do.

29

'I've told you. A deal that didn't come off.'

'Something to do with your shop?'

'Yes. They were auctioning the stuff from a villa on the Riviera. Everything. Piece by piece. But it was all rubbishy. What about you? Did you see your President?'

I cannot bear her smiling like that, as if to mask her lie. She has lit a cigarette: Legs tucked under her, not caring what she shows, she still has that inevitable rightness that accompanies her in her every move, she being so apart from what surrounds her.

'Will you take me somewhere? Into the country?'

I am enchanted as I watch her dressing again: the precise actions, the break in them as she answers a question, with lipstick held ready, say.

'What I don't understand,' I said, 'is why you didn't tell me you had to go there.'

She looked at me steadily, as if she was reading a sight-testing card with her eleven-tenths penetration.

'Why didn't you tell me?' I repeated.

She was silent, and I felt she was searching for an answer.

'Look, darling. Let's agree about one thing: neither of us must badger the other. And let's kiss on that.'

That was enough to satisfy me: all my uncertainties went on her lips. I had learnt to ask for no explanations, in the same way as Joan never questioned me about the evenings that I spent away from her: a new way of loving that we were trying together.

'We could drive along the Po, have some of their fish.'

'All right, let me take you.'

She sat herself at the wheel of her car. We slipped

into the motorway for Piacenza when it was already midday. The heat was terrific and the wind of our speed rushed through the open windows to flutter her scarf like a white mane. I have always liked watching her when she drives, her straight profile, broken by the sun-glasses, her sure movements that are almost masculine, while her clothes are so youthful, girlish.

We spoke of trifles, of where we would spend the holidays, perhaps at her place at Portovenere, and it gave me an illusion of well-being to find I had become once more like so many other men who whizzed by boldly with their women at their side, tenderly holding Joan's hand that hung down by the gear lever.

To judge by the number-plates and the paunches, no one was there in the third lane but peaceful Germans, perhaps with ten thousand well-tried men, you could have taken all Germany at that moment.

'Still in a mood?'

We laughed, hungry by this time, and coming out between the toll-boxes, headed for the river. I knew a couple of places where you could eat out under the trees, fried fish with that white wine of theirs, but they were both crowded out by fishers in sweat-shirts, bawling families, cars spewing radio programmes.

'Sorry, Joan, I'd no idea . . .'

'It doesn't matter. Let's sit over there.'

We took seats at a table on the edge of all the jollity, and Joan began to make fun of me.

'These are your people, aren't they? They're humanity, and you want to save them, that right?'

I let her joke about this, as I always did, there was nothing much to take exception to, after all, the meal was bad and we quickly left.

31

'I've just remembered. There's a place near Parma that I'd like to visit with you.'

Sabbioneta, on the estate of Vespasiano Gonzaga. I had never been there myself. We ran along straight deserted roads, between rows of high poplars, and an hour later we were passing under the gate where the drawbridge would have been raised behind us once, and a dead city showed before us, shut in grassy walls, with empty streets and squares in the heat of the siesta hour.

That solitude, the noise of footsteps between sun and shadow, under the porticos, made us feel ourselves again. We took shelter from the flaming noon inside the church of Sant'Assunta, sat on a bench in the cool that smelt of mould, incense and painted angels.

'What a joke, to see you in church.'

'If you want, I'll marry you,' I whispered to her.

We were about to go out again and I kissed her, shielded by a confessional. A piece of exorcism against something that would come and break this perfection. From the high vaults, saints eyed us, happy baroque creatures, they too, almost identical to the ones of your childhood, contemplated amid the organ music that brought tears to your eyes, and you waited for a sign from the carved Christ above the altar, with a desire to do good which ravished you, and the columns of Santa Francesca Romana shook with the deep roar of all the bass-stops in unison, 'Lord, I am not worthy', the tongue stretched to the miracle, the incense that waved up from the thuribles like a drug, real tears streaking your cheeks, whispering 'forgive me' for that hand which was making you a man, joined as it was this moment with the other in prayer, and mother comes back to knock at the bathroom door impatiently, that murderous hand that Mucius Scaevola plunged in the glowing charcoal—so, our reading book—before Porsenna, a sinful pleasure enjoyed in a body that was the abode of God, I shall indeed be a temple of purity, help me, Lord, and at night you fought you measured yourself against that hand turned into demon, the sacred host raised on high, and you two paces away in a white surplice held the incense-boat, or the large missal, ready to die for them, pierced by a sword, thirsting for eternity in the enervating torment of the sheets.

Outside, the light blinded us. The bronze bells in the tower were striking four, the air quivered with the cicadas' din and we were in the square where the old hospital is, inside the temple with the skylight, and finally carried away by the court theatre, we ran along the gallery of the Monstress, like phantoms in a Venetian spell of perspective, of harpsichords, perhaps the lagoon under us there, between the brick arches, and this was peasant Emilia, the region of woollen cloaks, of mists, but really it was the one overthrown by the summer.

A sort of alarm takes you when you study the photographs of yourself as a child: the innocent gaze, the half-open mouth as if you were on the watch for some omen of what you were going to become, and now you know that it is nothing more than regret for the high and the noble that has gone from our lives, certainty in knowing that no one will ever again give us back ourselves as we were, full of pride but with little wisdom, the prospect of a setback electrified us, gave us double the strength, we threw off every trace of cynicism, yielding, cowardice, not even the idea of death terrified us, as long as it was glorious some way, for we had nothing to repent of as yet, neither regrets nor remorse, happy to sacrifice yourself still spotless, untouched by the petty cares of adulthood.

Like that for my father and mother too: blasted at their only instant of love, in his rented room in Viale Piave, that afternoon in 1929, the unrepeatable moment of their existences, and at the paper yesterday you were asking and looking for that photograph, to understand why, you were walking with them on the new dust of Bratsk, Siberia, with women just out of the supermarkets, workmen pushing little trolleys, the same proud, sunburnt features, the wind that fluttered the headscarves of the girls knotted at the back of their neck, someone in boots, many in boots, and mud-stuck pebbles out of excavators, the smell of wet plaster, of varnish, and the lowering sky of the tundra, the black and white shoes of my father, the same soft, loose-falling jackets, frail birch-trees newly planted, I walked with them in a world unspoilt, them as they were, people who had not seen Rome in their lives just as the others will never see Moscow, in an uncorrupt world, in which he carried his Moorish disease with him, fever, the plague of taste, in the powder scattered among the hair on his chest, meanwhile the photographer drags his stand round towards us, with the Doge's palace in the back-

34

ground, as if we were sucked in by the ochre walls, by the kindly façade of Maria Luigia, and you keep your grip on the handlebars of your little bike, proud of these two people standing behind you, proud of the world that at twenty you will loathe, that only today on this bench beside Joan takes on meaning, in the voice of Tito Schipa, the deceptive Sunday peace of our lovely country, great with a greatness that is barely monumental, but which my father, having worked out the numbers of hours of overtime and of the white uniforms on the dais, will take for real.

'I remember there was a platform at the end of the avenue and people with baskets,' I said. 'Wait: a celebration for the wine harvest.'

Joan listened, absorbed, this place of rediscovered memory, with other children and prams and soldiers walking out, the same pebbles as thirty years previous.

'Perhaps for them it was really a happy period, d'you believe that?'

They sang let's live without sadness, live without any more jealousy, with towering fez-like party hats on, never supposing the bomb on Hiroshima will be, the extermination of millions, final solutions, the strength of that people you would have called 'perfidious Albion', at the railway station, while the trainload of Alpine infantry went off from the platform, in a subdued outburst of tricolour paper-flags, to the rhythm of the band at the rail's end, and on the line right beside it, we stood looking out from our carriages, with sail-cloth caps on our heads, bound for the seaside camps, for one last summer of thoughtlessness.

'Look,' said Joan. 'A porcupine.'

The grace with which she balanced that bunch of quaking spikes on her hand horrified me.

'For God's sake, put that disgusting thing down.'

She kissed me on the mouth, glad to obey me for once, on the bench where he and my mother would never have dared to.

'I shall take you to Busseto, to see Verdi's house.'

'Is that another of your memorable places?'

'No,' I said. 'Just so as we don't have to dine too early.'

It was six o'clock, and the heat drew up mists from the countryside. She stared at the landscape and licked her ice-cream cone.

'Joan, you never tell me about your work.'

'Well—it's not so interesting.'

I wanted to learn about her, not about fine iron and Chinese vases.

'I phoned you twice yesterday, at your shop. They told me you were out.'

I was making a mistake, to judge by her frown, and she took my hand.

We did not talk at supper either, in a transport café at Busseto, near a melon nursery, I was driving again when we headed back home, because onrushing car lights tired Joan out, or perhaps because all that sun had exhausted her, as it does a child, and on the motorway she leant her head on my shoulder. At the exit for Lodi which was indicated by an arrow under a light, I was tempted to go roaring on up the ramp. I told her.

'You could do it,' she said sleepily. 'If I had any urges like that, I'd get rid of them.'

36

'I would have smashed your car up and maybe you as well.'

She did not answer. We ran along the black ribbon, swallowing moths, in that state of bewilderment which always comes when you revive childhood memories. We passed on to the fly-over. Once among the lights of the city, Joan shook herself.

'What's gone wrong?' she asked.

'Nothing, why?'

'Of course, something's wrong. I know you. Would you like us not to see one another for a while?'

I stopped at her entrance, but she did not ask me to come up.

'Joan . . .'

'Better not, you're tired.'

Then the big door closed behind her, as if on a girl who is engaged now.

The tall stem of the aloes, that yellow of prickly flowers, the dust of Spain, coming down on Calpe, in the car hired at Malaga, it was strange that the aloe should be there at the curve, looking as if it were made of cloth on that too blue sky, the solitary flower known on holidays, the main reason which now recurred to mind, as you rattled it out boldly on the typewriter keys, being your article on Gibraltar, and instead it spoke about the rock, the cannons and tunnels you had visited 'O.H.M.S.', touching, and no more, on that clumsy whale-shape which bulks on the horizon, and there was something so different to be written, if that were allowed, but a paper is a paper, they pay you for things like this, a description done in local colour, with photographs, to be ready by the evening.

So, remember this, if this split in your living torments you, as you say, to the point where, Engels pushed open his study door, and sat on the swivel chair, and there was the little money-box at his back containing all the plus-value in new sovereigns, the din of looms and whirling spindles from the nearby shack, My God, he must have thought, though, to be exact, what he said was, 'damn'd Commerce', all the chimneys of Manchester smoking, little Lancashire girls in the vast window-barred halls, and corporals in bowlers and braces, and then Engels took the ledger which he had on the desk before him and wrote opposite the date of 4th September, 1864: remember to send money to Karl.

On my own desk diary I could read: remember to send flowers to J. Uneasily, because she had not rung yet although I had sent the flower-boy round to her 'express', and that was hours earlier. I forced myself to remember, going over my notes, the colour Gibraltar has, the high Victorian bastions, and then the centre of town with Elizabeth in the window and bobbies who spoke Andalusian, aware that, really, I was wondering about Joan. And just as in dreams, when it is the telling details rather than the happening itself that strikes us, the colour of an object, its unusual shape, the absence of shadow, so now my relationship with her appeared before me in a series of distorting mirrors.

If I tried to define it, Joan escaped me at once, impatient of every classification, I could not find adjectives that would evoke her in the part of myself that was still lucid, that asked the other part, lost to reason now, what had made me surrender. In fact, the thought struck me as I forgot for a moment the Union Jack which for two centuries has waved over the Moorish castle and the bay: that I had set Joan in a pure dream of childhood, peeping through the bars of the gate at the villa in Valbrona, the little countess Alice who sways back and forwards on the swing, the dry leaves on the elm are shining still, just as she drags her feet to stop herself, on the gravel, she stops because you are staring at her, and then starts swinging again, gracefully, a few steps away, until there comes a braying from the express bus at the curve, quite suddenly, and the big hound rushes up to the gate, snarling, but you know that the appointment is simply put back, and one day the gate will open for you and you will walk on the well-cropped grass with the step of the executioner, as if you were overcoming a fortress, instead of which it will be revenge, and barely that, for hours spent beyond the wall that closes this in, where you thrilled as the lizards darted under the Virginia creeper.

So, on one occasion, looking in at the gate, you pronounced her name loudly: Alice, the boys round about had told you that was her name, and at once a woman's voice was raised to question, from the garden-seat where she sewed, and the dog threw itself against the bars, and you retreated, shamefaced, a thief surprised who hides his hands behind his back, and does not know how long he will have to walk before, one day, he does take off his shoes to enter a house, 'Take off your shoes', as you visit the Gandhi

39

memorial, and go forward stocking-soled over the mats. Then Alice shook her head, her light ringlets flailing the air, and called the dog back with the same natural authority as Joan. Now nothing was left for you but to go along, all the more so because the boys round about are talking about her in the churchyard when evening falls, a motorbike with a trailer is roaring up, and the racket covers their last words, and I only see the gesture they make, to show how Alice is made underneath, and the tallest of them says: with a hole in her, and he guffaws, with a hole in her, they all repeat, and you know what hurts you: the possibility that it is true, there's the most stabbing thing, that a woman-child of old lineage, as Joan is, may be the bitch you are looking for, already enjoyed, right there on the floating throne of her roof-garden, shameless queen of the castle who does not even answer or turn her head if I call up to her from the street.

'It's me,' I said. 'Could you send some one down to open up for me?'

'Where are you?'

The tone of her voice, for a fleeting instant, seemed uncertain.

'Down here in the bar near your place.'

Going out of the bar, I crossed over to wait at her entrance. Her maid opened the door, and we went up in the lift together. Joan was having a bath, passing her bedroom I glimpsed her squat leather grip, the one she used for short journeys, plumped on the bed.

I was tempted to go up to it, perhaps it still had the airline tab looped to its handle. Or question her maid. God but I was losing my head. But Joan knew that I would not do anything like that, just as she would never raise her voice to speak to me from another room, and in fact she came in serenely, in all her glory.

'You're glorious, Joan.'

'Hullo, darling.'

Her embrace reassured me, impetuous and so brief.

'You seem to have come out of a bath of roses.'

'As a matter of fact, I've had a terrible day. Have you dined?'

'In a snack-bar, as soon as I got out of the paper.'

'How did things go in Gibraltar? When did you get back?'

'At six. What about you?'

'I've told you: a lousy day.'

She went over to the drinks counter, came back with a bottle and glasses.

'It's your birthday today,' I said. 'Many happy returns.'

'Oh, you've remembered the date.'

'Of course. And I did send you flowers.'

There was a silence that seemed to tell bewilderment on her side.

'Pity you haven't seen them. I had them sent along to your shop, as soon as I arrived, from the airport.'

She took the glass from my hand so I could kiss her.

'I've been out all day. I'm sorry. How was I to guess?'

It was the first time I had sent her flowers, a bit of

weakness which had immediately blown up in my face.

'You must have sweltered on Gibraltar.'

'It was pretty hot. How was it with you?'

'As you've probably heard by now, it's been no joke here either.'

'I mean, how was it in that place you went to . . ?'

She emptied her glass, lowered her eyelids a moment, glowing.

'It doesn't matter where I go,' she whispered. 'I'm only waiting to be back here, like this, the two of us.'

The telephone was ringing.

'Aren't you going to answer it?'

'You're here,' she shrugged, in triumph.

It is so hard to resist her, when she puts her hands to the side of my face and strokes my cheeks, gazing at me, exalted and intent, as if in farewell, and there was something you wanted to add before you fell down at her goddess knees: I commend myself to the mercy of this court, I said in thought.

Brought up on textbook accounts of the battle of the Ebro, of the Republic of Ossola, and then up and down the Algerian *jebel*, or breathing through a length of cane as you lie submerged in the flooded paddy fields. For your country's sake, or for power, or an idea. To your sons, the glory and the riches. There are so many ways of fighting on, but one is the hardest: when you struggle to remain whole, trying to save your own gut and your convictions too, the lowest instincts, the unsated desires, along with the noble, the inspiring things that you expected from yourself. If it lasts long enough, this struggle can tear you to shreds, seeing that the Western imperialists are guilty of such provocation that serious measures must be taken against them (from the work already quoted). And you need not only a powerful regular army but a local militia as well, trained to fight in units, large ones, too, and there is a minute crab that pincers his way from the sand, more stubborn than a Red Guard as he makes for his hole that is right beside Joan's sun-glasses, and she is lying out immobile, half-naked and a little post-bath, in the great light of the early afternoon, at this little bay on the island of Palmaria, giving voice to an occasional thought with her eyes closed.

'I've been thinking that this is where you'll begin your book on Africa. I'll put a table at the window for you, and you'll work through the afternoon. In a fortnight you could do something, some part of it.'

'But I don't have my notes here,' I began. 'Where can I get the facts?'

I knew it was useless, she would not answer.

'Just for a change, doesn't it occur to you that I'm dying of hunger?'

'I'm going to dive in again.'

'O no, Joan. Please don't. You'll take another half hour to get dry.'

'You come in the boat, I'm swimming it.'

She put on her top again and vanished with a splash into the waves. I gathered up the books, the cigarettes, the papers, got into the boat, and in two pulls on the oars had made up with Joan. She threshed the swell with her perfect crawl-stroke in the stretch of sea that cuts the little island off from Portovenere, and you could make out the windows of her house, on the sixth floor of that red-plastered block, with an air of casual peace about it.

'Clamber aboard,' I shouted. 'There's a whole shoal of stinging jellyfish!'

She stopped to take breath, scanned the water around her, then protested in amusement.

'You go ahead and get us a table in the shade.'

Her staying powers always impressed me, formidable despite her slight arms, as if she had done nothing else for years, in preparation for a shadowy contest that was perhaps no more than this: that I should admire her making her way, stubbornly, in the boat's wake; but it could have been something else unknown to me.

On the breakwater I would gather her to me again, dripping, her eyes shining from the water, her girl's bosom still heaving with that exertion.

'How are you getting on? Managing to work?'

What more could I ask? The little strait in front of me, the green patch of Palmaria on my right, the crystallised twigs which Joan had placed on the table for me, a perfect skyline for blackening a few sheets on my portable.

'Joan, you go out: take the car and drive to Lerici and buy the papers.'

'No I won't. I like to hear you working.'

She is at my back, stretched out on her front upon the bed, perhaps pretending to read.

44

'Sorry,' she added. 'This gives you too matrimonial a feeling, doesn't it?'

I was trying to explain on the page before me why Africa had disappointed every hope of ours, and what were the reasons for this destiny she had of being subordinate, but, quite aside from the distraction in the landscape, it was hard work trying to put this into words with Joan beside me, fragrant with sun oil, with spices, with barbary vessels, and they were the fishing boats which at dusk go out on the sea with nets and lamps.

'One of these nights,' I said, 'I want to go out with them, and draw up the sardines.'

'You didn't answer my question. Is this too matrimonial?'

I heard the motors stutter alive, while the boats moved on under us, in Indian file along the canal. Of course, we had even gone as far as saying, having summed up our respective experiences, that we would never live together, and here I was, all the same, in her lovely house at Portovenere newly done up with lime and ceramic, at the top of that twisted staircase that is Liguria, and without noticing it we were giving definite form to vague plans of an earlier time, formations in the game that then had seemed to us too perfect to come about.

'I was thinking,' I said, 'of those mornings at Porta Vittoria.'

'Now you've got to think about your book.'

I saw the vessels filing round the cliff where the little church of Saint Peter's is, and then point, minute now, out to sea. One day, this too, an everyday image, would combine with others, similar or little different,

45

to make up the one reminder of a summer, just as of those other mornings nothing was left but the first of them, when we went up the stairs, excited as two youngsters, especially Joan: her raincoat, the headscarf wet with rain, but our gestures are grave, almost unsmiling, until the key turns in the lock, someone below had summoned back the lift, and it is as if they are after us, while we embrace finally in a hall that seems full of books, a narrow passage, the bedroom, as if we had got down at the station from different trains, Joan, her mouth tasting of rain, on a November morning, intimate, the smell of wet silk knotted under her chin.

'Up to the last minute,' she pants, 'I thought I wouldn't make it.'

It is the hands that talk, every time between eleven and noon, with every supposition on the Afro-Asiatic question gone in a short taxi-ride, both living a fever which hardly will let us break apart even in the moment of undressing, you see what you are looking for in this delirious time with her, in the race against the passing minutes, Joan is your forbidden nun, your nun of Monza, that viceregal Lombard fever, now you, with your Arab blood, join yourself with this Spanish sex of hers which is the only one that exists, you would like to think yourself an emir's bastard, now you have rediscovered your history, and at the same time the coldness of her father, the Count, the spasms of her lover, Giangiacomo Mora, as they break the joints in his body so he can be tied to the wheel, the caress drawn out till it is torture, look and see how a woman is made, can that really be her, you ask yourself, and you threw yourself down on the pillow, came to the surface again among her hair.

'Joan, a half hour's gone.'

We were putting on our disguises again, having climbed back up from the depths.

'This brother reporter of yours,' she adds, 'will he give you the key again?'

Nothing but sky to be seen through the windows, and roofs shining with rain, if we look out over the balcony.

'Darling, we've messed up the quilt.'

With all the things we had to tell one another: if she were free, deciding to break, talk, put an end to it. Because someone had told her husband they had seen her come out of the hotel, and she admitted it, she had stepped inside to pull up a stocking.

'I'd like a house like this, just for myself, on top of the roof, small like this, with everything in disorder.'

We spoke with our arms wound round one another, looking out at the rain, as if we were 'the betrothed' in the bedroom to be.

'You'd visit me sometimes, when you come back from a trip.'

And suddenly she presses me tight, stung by a thought.

'But the truth is I'm afraid.'

I say Joan to her, drink in her breath while she has breath, for her to say that and she a warrioress.

'I'm afraid for our love. It could drag on like this, nothing great about it, from one bed to another. Without us ever really sharing, really talking . . .'

She turned on her side away from me, as if to hide something I should not see, perhaps tears of bitterness, because after a few seconds I hear her sniff and clear her throat, face to the pillow.

'Joan. Come here.'

At once, because in a month it will be Christmas, a new infantry brigade will come ashore in the Mekong delta, and we shall be surrounded, armed with nothing but our make-believe.

'It's the same for me, Joan. I can't bear hiding things any longer.'

This civilisation of bells, as once more and again, I clutch her and roll with her into the void, noon is ringing at Porta Vittoria, it is noon on every watch. I wanted to say if it were to rain for days, then to keep in one another's arms with the windows thrown wide, before they open fire on us, but instead we are putting ourselves in order again, each looking for scattered garments, the debris of our battle.

'Oh, Joan, I believe that . . .'

Her eyes in the bathroom mirror sparkled.

You said then: 'We'll go somewhere on a trip, I'll take a day's leave, we'll find the way.'

In five days, by setting myself to work every afternoon, as Joan wanted, I compiled the first thirty pages of what was to be my book on Africa, giving the thing a better shape as I went along. It was to be limited to Black Africa, and I might even call it *De Affrica*, though the old chronicler's term did not cover that: and I was not thinking of a book given over to abstract considerations, but a narrative in which the no-event of the black Continent's liberation, her revolutions and counter-revolutions, would emerge from everything I had seen of flies upon eyelids, by the hundred, on the eyelids of black children, and then the pantomime costumes, and gold watches bending to eat from enamelled bowls, sentries in white gloves frozen at the present-arms, that morning in Port Mombasa, as a shoe rolls down the gangway, the shoe of the President's wife, and she surrounded by ministers in morning dress, a desperate and bloody puppet theatre.

'Bloody?' said Joan.

Our impressions of Africa never square, if you leave out the colour of the landscape, or the swimming pools of the various hotels.

'I am not suggesting that the Congo is an open wound on your conscience, Joan.'

'Is it on yours?'

It was getting hot. Half-naked, tapping on my portable at the window, the closeness of the afternoon made the sweat run down me, Joan was on the bed, occupied with something as always, allowing for the attitude of Neo-colonialism, for the irony in her gaze.

'Listen to this record.'

'Sorry. I'll have to go out. I'm out of cigarettes.'

I slipped on a shirt and went down. I felt the urge to stretch my limbs. I went into the tobacconist's, got cigarettes, there was a selection of fine, coloured views of the place, so I took one and wrote out a silly phrase for Joan. Now I would have to post the thing. I crossed the little square. At the breakwater they were tying up a huge three-master, the woodwork above decks all beautifully waxed, and the usual group of idlers were watching the operation and the sailors throwing the ropes.

I stayed myself, seated on a step some way off, to watch the regal personages land. I lit a cigarette and Africa began to drift away with its futile questions of apartheid, as Cortez followed by his men placed his foot on the shore, because the galleon flew the Spanish flag, and a question occurred to me: were they not perhaps the last of yesterday's world rather than the first of the overriding new age?—a rhetorical question with no answer to it, which filled my eyes with liquid blue in the sun's blaze, forgetting that I too, by a mistaken transference of instinct, had been on the other side five centuries earlier.

Perhaps I would not have dared to confide it even to Joan. Well then, it was a morning of autumn mist, on one of the sentry walks on the castle walls, the city itself was invisible from up there; and walking like this, enjoying the privilege of being alone by the massive battlements and towers, something metallic flashed in the fog, the sun getting through, I could not tell whether it was glass or the fittings on one of the cars in the square, perhaps going round the monument, but, of course, French troops who were moving up with carts and siege-engines against our Duke Francesco, and so strong was the feeling of greatness in this that you were being forced to take sides in a flash, and in a flash your instinct has chosen for you, before any question of class struggle arises, and everything you are takes on the shape of a Milanese gentleman, perhaps painted by Andrea Solario with the suspect droop of the mouth, the gaze that never leaves the observer whichever way he go, the eyes of a young lord, an insolent vassal with page-style hair that is reddish in tint, perhaps portrayed by Ambrogio De Predis with the same lights and shadows to the face that you are rediscovering in your own, the prominent cheek-bone, that proud air that makes you take up your sword, and finally you are aware which side it is you would have thrown your weight on, with the princes, I tell you, behind the standard of the great Sforza serpent, a playmate of Ludovico's, the enlightened adviser of Francesco, reciting poems or penning diplomatic dispatches, how could you have dreamt of a revolt?

Well then, you were standing in a cutaway of those Ghibelline battlements looking out on the smokestone void, the traffic below blinded by the mist, and a lute melody rose in your veins, the crackling of a hundred fire-arms from the glacis, in the roaring of our Lombard men: the Duke alone stood unruffled, as he visualised the coming fight, with his velvet cap on his head, as red as Bembo saw it, the huge rings on his fingers indicating the points at which the enemy, down there, would site his catapults and mortars.

And at last the Duke said: If we were at the beginning of summer, I would agree with what Ludovico has wisely said, but as we are near to the inconveniences of winter, it seems to me we should take the advice that season and necessity offers us. And in these short days it will be necessary to get winter quarters ready for our soldiers, and take back the Cremona district, which was our granary once, and now is the

Venetians', and wrest from the enemy at least two crossing-points on the river Adda, by which the eastern part of Milanese territory is assailed and plundered every day. But above all we have to consider that these French soldiers who are not used to rain and cold will not be so active with their weapons then as ours will be.

And a silence followed these words. You savoured the taste of being among the men best at managing arms and at finding the exact word, perhaps to be the Duke's legate one day, raised up in the refulgence of his power, and although you knew nothing of Joan, already you were looking for her among the ladies of the castle, velvet to tear away in a guardroom, the laces of her bodice broken with your two hands, and outside the cannonballs already whistle, the mouths of bronze levelled at the corners, where you stand now at this loophole, now here's a time to live, of arque-buses fired by wicks, the silk-workers, the mob that does not demand an end to bondage, the golden age of the Duchy of Milan, of might made right, with all the odours under the dress, an age for her, always, for Joan.

'Is that you? You've had me worried.'

'Why, what's happened?'

She looked almost shattered.

'Didn't you notice? You've been out for more than an hour!'

'What about it?'

'O nothing. Only—you could have told me in advance.'

'Fair enough, Joan, but I'm here now.'

'You're here but something could have happened to you, you don't understand . . .'

'I'm sorry, I couldn't foresee this.'

Seeing so much alarm on her face touched me, even if I was a thousand miles then from guessing the reason for her uneasiness. We dined in a place that was very smart, one Joan knew, near Fiascherino.

'Did you come here with your husband?'

'Why?' She spoke calmly.

We always avoided talking of our matrimonial pasts, a tacit understanding that I had violated this evening.

'Sorry, Joan, I was joking.'

'Well, find something else for your humour.'

She smiled as she does, not in the least amused, wrinkling the corners of her mouth so slightly. I looked at her slim fingers, their sunburnt tinge upon the white of the tablecloth, the glow of the brilliant on her ring finger, as she chopped bread into crumbs with her nail.

'You didn't understand, did you, why I was concerned?'

What she was saying seemed to cost her a great effort.

'But there is one thing you must know. You've not to ask me any more questions.'

She paused as if to gather strength.

'They can hit me through you.'

I was pouring wine for her.

'Who can?'

'I told you now: don't ask any more questions.'

I watched her without thinking out a phrase, without any precise thought in my head, suddenly aware how unreachable she was, how secret, the same feeling I had experienced when, one evening, in a friend's house, I had approached her for the first time. We did not go dancing. I took her home, in haste, and we made love till two in the morning. But Joan revealed nothing more.

Because this is our battle, the only real one left us, arms about one another, after a careful reconnaissance of the terrain, throats dry, saliva all gone, working out new types of ambush, according to age-old principles, which my father himself had put into practice on the body of her, the dressmaker he disarmed that peaceful Sunday in the summer, there had been the approving of the list of deputies designated by the Grand Council of the Nation, when everyone seemed sunk in a pleasant torpor, as my mother was in those bony arms of his, not yet guessing the number of her losses, lying back as Joan is now, her side against mine, listening to the night silence of the sea.

'Are you asleep?' she called out after a little while.

'No,' I answered.

Gusts of the breeze blew out the curtains from time to time. I felt the softness of her shoulder beside my arm which was bent back below the pillow. I thought of all the things that she kept guard over, the obscure things, even while we lay unspeaking in one another's arms, and an abrupt stab of pain, piercing as the spasm of a nerve disease, took the breath from me.

'I was thinking,' Joan said. 'It was lovely sending me that postcard from here of all places.'

'This time tomorrow we'll be thinking: if only we were here.'

'Unless you're in bed with some silly girl,' she said, pursuing a thought.

'But, of course, darling.'

Then she fell asleep, naturally, closed up in her impenetrable anguish, leaving me to frame absurd hypotheses as to its nature, the sort of thing I had done before only at the period of Uncle Peter, tacking together snatches of conversation and hints of something frightening.

I know we were sitting at table, at table with Uncle Peter and Mrs Miriam whom I could never bring myself to call 'Aunt'. They had arrived that evening from Naples on the express, and the hotel, Uncle Peter was explaining, the hotel in Naples suits us very well indeed, and that's that, let's change the subject, but you know perfectly well what it's all about, and take you, Mrs Miriam had just said, who are you to laugh at missionaries when you've never been in Africa, and with every gesture of hers the gold bracelets at her wrist jingle (they were earned at Asmara, Eritrea, in the years of the Empire), her large, fleshy arms, lucky no one else guesses how much I have understood: about their hotel, and the 'crusading' life peeress, that damned life peeress, says Uncle Peter, and at that point I was in my parents' bedroom trying on the suède shoes that Uncle Peter was casting off, and they were almost new, and my father was saying: Just you wait and see, *that* law will take a long time to pass, don't you worry, and meanwhile the precious stone on Uncle Peter's little finger fairly sparkled, restlessly up and down the room, apart from the problem of having to move one's 'personnel' every few months and the ever-rising cost of finding replacements, I am taking time to lace them up, then I walk a step or two in Uncle's shoes until my father is saying: What are you doing here, come back to the table and join the others, we're talking, you know, and only my mother didn't understand what purpose the two mirrors framed in Empire style are going to serve (Uncle had picked them up today at a bankruptcy sale), and you were on the point of shouting it to her, brutally, you there! wounded by their lost integrity, hurt by their capacity for low dealings which would infect us all, even through the thousand lire note Uncle would press into my hand, as soon as I had put his case into the boot of the eleven-hundred.

A stupid fact but newsworthy, one of those things that interest people so much, or perhaps it was a trap to try me out in new territory: in short, a student for the priesthood, who refused to wear the regulation clothes or, rather, regulation skirts.

'But listen, boss—why me of all people?'

'Robert's ill, and furthermore nothing better's come up in the last few days.'

I had to be exact, no digressions, the facts were all that was wanted. I went there with a photographer, that very morning, in the paper's own car. On the way we ran into mist, at the bridge over the Adda.

The town on the height was invisible, but when we entered the lane for Colle Aperto, where the seminary was, the sky opened to a warmish autumn sun. A caretaker came to open the gate.

'Our boarders are exercising,' the superintendent said.

We sat outside on the parapet of the boundary wall, looking towards the valley. I heard their shouts, their laughs, and even the local accent as they called for the ball.

'And where is our conscientious objector?' I asked.

'Please, please don't call him that: he is simply overwrought.'

He was in his room, cut off from the others—his gesture being such a serious matter—until the hierarchy decided what steps to take, and it would be a shame to expel him, with the excellent marks he had been getting.

'I think we'll take the opinion of a specialist.'

'What do you mean?'

'I mean, a psychiatrist. There's a professor of psychiatry near here who's very conscientious.'

The director joined us as we were walking in their grounds. The photographer had begun shooting film here and there, 'with the approval of his superiors', while the seminarists exerted themselves on both sides of a volleyball net. Their pitch was of concrete, not altogether straight, and the ball broke on it at unexpected angles. I stared at the long black skirts flying about in that ugly enclosure. I imagined how this must humiliate them as men and what the most forthright one among them must have suffered. Now he was under arrest. I asked if I could speak to him for a few minutes but the director said he was sorry, but he could not oblige me unless I had the written authority of this Diocese. Because we had to understand, we outsiders, that it was a very delicate matter. Once an instance of disobedience was reported in the press, where did it end? The most damaging thing of all, and this with regard to his brother seminarists, is that this young man should have turned the thing into a public scandal by writing to the papers and saying it was time to throw clerical dress way, in fact, it is only too clear that he has a screw missing somewhere . . .

They showed me round the place by way of compensation, a grey building that smelt of soup, dark halls, the refectory, one of their rooms with an iron bedstead and great patches of damp on the walls, all of them things that it was as well not to photograph.

'You have this craze for photographing everything, you people. But here we've nothing that's interesting enough: just poor bits of furniture, as you can see for yourselves.'

He kept on rubbing his hands, perhaps in his anxiety to see us gone. The superintendent listened with bent head, his hands thrust into the broad, black waistband. I observed that there was a television set, but they told me that the students were forbidden to watch it, the reason being that you get everything, these days, on the little screen too, ballerinas and not so much ballerina either.

'They have the library, come and see it, it's perfection.'

I went up to the shelves: there was not one novel on them, only sacred texts, tracts, the history of religions, the biography of Don Bosco, the Story of Art by Van Loon, what you get in prisons.

'They can do without some things,' the superintendent laughed, 'with all they have to study in dogma and theology.'

I was crushed. In my notebook all I had jotted were descriptive touches. I asked myself how the hell I'd make an article out of that. A bell in the courtyard rang on and on. The break was over, another hour of study was beginning. From the valley, deep in mist, there came at intervals the wailing hoot of an express bus.

'When will the psychiatrist examine him?' I asked again.

They did not know, and in any case they would not have told me.

'Did he give any signs, before this, of being unbalanced?'

'Last year. He kept some French periodicals hidden under his mattress. It was the superintendent who found them.'

'Pornographic?' I asked.

'Worse than that: publications dealing with the worker priests, loose sheets and manuscripts too. He was going to use these to write a book . . .'

They would not show me what had been seized, but I knew the sort of thing it was. I knew too that it was time to get away before the director noticed that our photographer was snapping him on the sly. The sports pitch was deserted. Through the ground-floor window, I saw the seminarists bent over the desks, the ruddy-cheeked faces of them, country people, already old at twenty; living in a silence right outside time, that, in spite of myself, I found fascinating, comparable to the day on which the Duke bearing down on the enemy, drew all his men up in formation. And all the pairs on horseback who had jousted together that day, he divided up into a hundred and twenty squadrons, each with more than a hundred and twenty-five people on horseback, and so that these could be more readily commanded, he divided them, taken all together, into five parts, or five columns. And he desired that the first of these columns in which his own family rode along with the flower of his ablest men and tried veterans, should attend on him at all times, and he gave the charge of managing it and leading it to Ruberto and Gasparo of Vimercato. The second he gave to Ludovico. The third to Caglione. The fourth to Tiberto. The last to King Renato. And to each one he assigned his share of infantry, as the thick mist swallowed us up again, on our way back to Milan, under a pall we could not escape. Alone, shut up in his room, the young seminarist I was not allowed to meet, was left to struggle with the greatness of his 'no'.

How long, I wondered, for him too. Luckily for me, Joan would be back from Portovenere inside forty-eight hours.

The phone woke me up with a start at two in the morning. I put on the light. I noticed there was great disorder and dust everywhere, as my daily woman had not turned up for a week, and at first I didn't realise that Joan was phoning from Milan.

'I've just arrived.'

'Why didn't you come to my place?'

'It was misty on the way here and one of my lights wouldn't work.'

We arranged to meet the next day. At one I left the paper and called at her shop to pick her up. Joan was in a great chafe. The heavy shutter had been lowered half-way, because she had to give instructions about dressing the window.

'I want to exhibit these two wrought-iron pieces and the Dutch still life between them.'

I liked watching her at her job because she always considered it pointless, like a game. The person who did what she said, moving furniture and hammering in nails was a colossus of a man called Marcel. I had always seen him in passing, when he was pulling down the shutter at night, or going off to deliver something in his motor-cycle van. I took advantage of a moment when Marcel had disappeared into the back-shop to kiss Joan on the back of her neck as she carefully dusted a figurine in Sèvres porcelain. I told her that it would have excited me to see her sitting back on her heels in her own shop window, among the velvets, the most precious object of all, and that I would stand there on the pavement enjoying the sight while she took off a stocking before my very eyes. She promised she would do it one day, as long as I behaved quite correctly, and finally she locked the entrance and we went out into the courtyard.

It was then that I caught sight of Marcel, in the back-shop, busy washing himself at a tap. He was in a sweat-shirt, his arms and shoulders figured all over with tattoos. I went a few steps towards him, pretending I had mistaken the way out; his back, from his shoulders right over to what showed of his neck, was flecked with scars.

'Where are you taking me to lunch?'

I wondered about that myself: where could I decypher this other message that chance had picked up for me.

Now on the scar-marked texture, which was like a landscape blasted by explosions, you could plainly see the traces of malignant sores; on the edges of their centres, the hard crusts that were close together, spent craters of the flesh, buttresses raised by the skin around the tubero-serpiginous syphiloderm of the trunk, the glittering, tortured flashes of the whole surface.

ИЭМ, a senseless inscription painted on the frosted glass of a door, and you stare at it fascinated for a split second, and only when you go out of the lavatory, do you understand that it should be read from the other side, because, to be truthful, it was not the inscription you were trying to decode, but the illustrations, as coloured as the pages of an atlas, in this library where you have come to find an answer, the smell of disinfectant, a tap leaking somewhere, invisible, and you rediscover dark ancestral ties, the infinite number of childhood associations that are permeated by white chinawear and needs, by running water, sex and indecency, the ridge of your penis in this cool that seems to come from the lysol itself, and today those repellent shoulders, Marcel's back, a pit into which you could fall, newly opened up to all the savage possibilities: and since the ulceration is produced as a rule in syphilitic sores that have not been treated, I could deduce from this that the man came from the lowest depths of society, had been, say, a cook aboard a Greek trawler, a boarding-house keeper at Tangiers, a drug pedlar on the Canebrière, a deserter from the Legion, a brute warder at Mauthausen, but that whatever he had been, Joan was in danger now.

There was a kind of heater beside the latrines, a staircase which went down darkly to a basement, a group of pipes plastered together which ran the whole length of the corridor. I kept looking at the inscription, I read ИƎM., as I wondered whether Joan was informed about his past, or whether he himself, Marcel, naked to the waist, had shown her his scars and tattoo markings, who knows even the number he was given as an inmate, stamped in indelible ink under his armpit.

Suddenly, without any momentous event occurring, my life had reached a turn, was at an unknown opening, and perhaps Joan alone kept the secret of it, in her abrupt departures, like the last time she had gone to Paris; in the groundless anxiety for my safety she had expressed at Portovenere; and in that second mysterious absence on her birthday; and now through Marcel, placed, by chance, at her side, with his repellent back, ready to harm her at the first opportunity, or perhaps to protect her like a bodyguard, to save her, he, the emblem of horrors, from the same unknowable risks that tormented me.

I began to wonder where Marcel had sprung from, and by what ways Joan had come to engage him, though I could never have asked her about him. Because I too would not discuss one part of myself:

the region of my daily life that was made up of meetings with my daughter, my difficult relations with a woman who had been my wife, humiliating money troubles which Joan would not have understood in any case, things we never discussed, private ground that did not belong to our common history. But not lies, because this had been our greatest conquest, honesty to the point where we would tell aloud unpleasant thoughts we had had about the other, a fierce competition of sincerity that must have helped us.

Because of this, her reactions now struck me as all the more unnatural. Like an itch which is inflamed by scratching, uneasiness grows as soon as we probe it to discover its source. The present becomes unintelligible, and memory, the past that you so stubbornly interrogated, added if anything new reasons for doubt, incredible possibilities. I wrapped myself in new enchantments.

No love is complete without caution, complicity, secrecy. I had been the one to instil these into Joan, a year previous, when she had been alarmed by continuous disturbances on her phone: suggesting that her husband could have had a recording device installed in it, one supplied by a private detective agency, and so we would have to speak in code, as if engaged on the sort of conspiracy they have perfected at Peking in the schools for sabotage.

'Can't you come out straightaway? I want to see you.'

I had explained that it was impossible, and then it

was something quite new for her to phone me in the forenoon from a bar near the paper.

'Listen,' I said, 'we can meet at three, near the clock.'

'We'd better not. He'll be going about that part just then, I'm sure of it.'

'All right then, at Silver's. At half past two. Can you manage that?'

'I'll invent some story or other.' She paused. 'You know, I've got bad news.'

At Silver's, which is to say at Silvia's, a popular restaurant with bedrooms upstairs, situated not far from the race-course, or near the clock, a euphemism for the room in Corso Matteotti that looked out on a street clock, kindly erected by the authorities of Milan: this second place was in a tailoring establishment which ran side-lines that were nothing if not discreet. So the trembling for something risked, for violated conventions, is increased by this new hazard of choosing, every so often, the time and place of the attempt, having studied the enemy's behaviour, and the lie of the land, although it is perfectly clear by now that terrorism in cities can play no decisive role, and on the contrary sometimes precipitates trouble of a political nature, because the least negligence can lead to ambush, perhaps in the very moment that you are sucking all the honey from a brief meeting, they will knock on the door, a few imperative raps, alarmed, then, we shall look at one another without daring any gesture, it is he who is mounting the stairs, and he will surprise us looking so ridiculous, paralysed, your hands frozen stiff upon Joan's shoulders, listen, there's something I must explain, you will say, and the vileness of it will grow into a roar.

I had left the office to have a bite in a snack-bar. I went to the place often, and every time, sitting at the counter, one back among so many lined up along the stools, you expect the burst of firing from the street. So I was forced to turn round, every so often, and see beyond the window-glass the face of the hungry man with the knotted muffler just as he is in Prévert's poems, you would like to call him, signal to him, offer him one of these unappetising dishes, and you make out his breath that mists the window, and perhaps he can sense the music coming through the loud-speaker as well as the smells from the grill: perhaps it is because of this that you expect the burst of firing, feel the bullets penetrate between your ribs while you sip iced beer, you have the selfsame fear that gangster had till he was struck down in the barber's shop, his face still soaped and the white towel at his chin, reddening as if it were blotting paper, or like this pizza splashed with tomato, see, you do have hallucinations, so I kept telling myself from that time on.

At a quarter past two that afternoon I had had to switch on my headlights. The mist was even thicker at the opening of the broad, tree-lined avenue. I drove around the square almost by memory alone, her car was there, no distance away, in a little clearing where the cottage-like stables begin. I parked beside hers, and noticed the traffic ticket which Joan had trailed around for about a week, quite unworried, stuck there under the wipers, until the next fall of rain destroyed it. On the driving seat lay her gloves, her sun-glasses, old papers which were part of the disorder which she alone could dominate.

'Have you been waiting long?'

She turned her little face that wore a grave smile. Thrown back on the chair, her fur coat trailed on the floor. Behind the espresso boiler Silver was already preparing two coffees for us.

'Hullo,' she had murmured, putting out her lips.

'Well, what's been happening? Would you rather we went upstairs?'

She shook her head: and you should know by now that she never likes things to be so hurried.

'You told me on the phone that you had news for me.'

Joan looked at me close, a depthless gaze which prepared me for the worst.

'Promise you won't get angry.'

She put her open hand on the tablecloth, so I could take it in mine.

'Tell me,' I said, pressing her fingers, not unaware of the romantic pose we held, or of the pallor of her wrists as they lay on the red haloes from the wine glasses.

'Well?'

'Nothing: I'm pregnant.'

What would this city be like, you wondered, us, the houses, our story, if the skyline were different. Not these tender mountain ridges, ashen in the February sky that shines beyond the window of this bedroom, one like so many, only this one is not to vanish from memory, beyond the door Joan is beginning to count one, two, three, four, but different features in the picture: perhaps with sugar-cane plantations, rubber forests, the rugged upsweeps of a sierra or a *jebel*, in place of this cloister of ash-coloured mountains, it would have been different, you were saying—Joan with thick white woollen stockings on her feet, because by now the anaesthetic was working in her—aware, too, of this natural mediocrity, and of the alpine calling of our city, of the melancholy of the lakes at its back, aware of my mother's eyes which end at Vienna, as if of a hereditary illness, in a distant flowing of genes and chromosomes, of busy spinning-girls, of Hapsburg bayonets, the coil of voices and echoes, and you shudder at the sudden rattle of polished steel on glass, the knocking of a basin, and now there is a river of blood, past and present legible at last, not words: blood at last, and it is she who pays for a moment's abandon for both of us, probably you will say a good many tender words to her, afterwards, but now what gnaws you is the certainty that my father, a man of honour, refuses to agree to this, even although she had already taken steps to deceive her mother with the signs of a regular blood-discharge, with linen borrowed from a girl-friend, left to soak in the lavatory pan, she confided this to him to set his heart at rest, the second Sunday in June, on a bench in the gardens at Montemerlo, near the ice-cream stall.

'You can come in now, right inside.'

She was beginning to regain consciousness, covered by her own fur coat on the vast double bed where they had operated on her, and you sat beside her on a false Empire-style chair, curling the fringe of the bedspread between your fingers.

'Joan, it's me.'

68

I had taken my handkerchief to wipe a film of sweat from her brow. I did not dare bend down and kiss her, because you kept looking at the dust of the public gardens, after he had asked you once again if you were quite sure, and together you had gone over the tally of days, starting from that Sunday in the boarding house in Viale Piave, unsuspecting as they both were of every trap in the calendar. And then you would have been dissuaded from the alternative, supposing you had considered it for a moment, by the news item there in the paper of three women arrested 'for criminal acts against maternity', one of them, the twenty-year-old washerwoman, Teresa Seveso, having been subjected to illegal practices in an apartment not far away, in Via Plinio, upon payment of a hundred and fifty lire.

'I'd like to get away from here,' Joan murmured.

It had not been easy, for her who had had no pregnancy during her marriage, to stay lucid and reasonable and not succumb to instinct.

'Easy, Joan, you've got to rest.'

In the clear sunlight beyond the curtain lurked something like the dawn, the doctor came in to hand me the bottle with the drops that I was to give her every six hours to avoid haemorrhage, he was carrying his coat and his hat, his little case, he gave her strict advice about not moving for another hour. But Joan drew herself up and sat on the bed the moment he went out.

'Let's leave, you'll have things to do at the paper.'

'Behave yourself. And don't worry.'

But no, she made me pass her stockings, then under-clothes, a forced smile on her lips the whole time. A clock ticked away on a mirror stand. I gazed at Joan, marvelling at her power of recovery, the way she had set herself to overcome the after-effects of the drugs, the sudden kicks of vomiting, the weakness and the nausea. Sitting there while she dressed again, I was working the fringe of the bedspread between my fingers with the guilty feeling in me that I was profaning something. I questioned the space dividing us (after he had taken my mother's hand between his and decided that I should come into the world), and could not define it. A strong bond, perhaps, or the limp complicity in a crime that had to be.

'How do you feel, darling?'

'Fine,' she smiled. 'Don't pull a face like that.'

I had risen up to take her face between my hands.

'Joan,' I called her name low. 'You really are the warrioress.'

Now I knew she could be that, yes could be anything at all, the thing furthest from my guesses which were abortive chiefly because they could not establish connections and proofs. The rules of behaviour which a man in his uncertainty tries to extract from experience (he can do this and no more) found no application with Joan. And just as, living in the city, we no longer lift our gaze to question the sky, feel the sun's blaze only on the leather of our car-seats, and a storm almost invariably catches us unawares, so Joan's moods, her lightning departures and returns, always surprised me, I was so unprepared for them.

'I don't understand it. Three days in Marseilles. To do what?'

'I have to see somebody, an antique dealer there.'

'And when will you be back?'

'In two days time. I'll take the plane from Nice. You can ring me at my hotel if you like. I'll be at the Astoria.'

I said nothing to that.

'Tell me you'll miss me.'

I said I would and hung up. As I looked from the bed, a horizon all of mist advanced towards me, the fog of an autumn morning, the everlasting view that is the background to the phone ringing, and it is her voice saying 'Good morning', an awakening so sweet, which you miss on your travels, and you go over the objects in the room, then other objects in other rooms, there's the roaring of a bus in the street, but things that are much nearer than these that you can touch, richer in meaning, the only ones to have any, in fact, thanks to the enormous physical distance that separates us from them; the wardrobe in a room with a shower, the plastic curtain patterned with flowers at Zagreb, or perhaps Belgrade, the terrifying distance between the bed and the window in the Grand Hotel at Saragozza, the tiny lift in the hotel at Athens, or, in Venice, the pink marble of the bath right on the Grand Canal, a catalogue of middling splendours and sanitary fittings, the soap wilfully slipping on the tilted surface of a washstand, and this is the boarding house at Marseilles, near the station, the first time you went there to report on the Legion, in winter, with the biting mistral that beat upon la Canebière, and so the name Astoria, pronounced by her, brought back without any straining the two days we would spend there.

*   *   *

The plaque, an oblong of darkened bronze, massive in its *artnouveau* frame, records that just here, one October day in '34, Alexander of Jugoslavia breathed his last, shot dead by a fanatic. Joan holds her fine chin up towards the lamp that shines on the inscription, at one of the first numbers of the Canebière, and you see so clearly how the light pours down on her, the police clear a way before them with their truncheons, Alexander is already lying back on the seat of the limousine with two holes in his uniform, only that it happened by day, at eleven o'clock in the morning to be exact, and the unlucky monarch was going in a procession of cars to the Hôtel de Ville. Long thin negroes come and go with lightning steps, the sick gaze of the Algerians rests on her, with obvious intentions, and she should not stop here, a couple of yards away from the cinema where the girls station themselves with glowing cigarettes, luckily there is Marcel standing on guard, behind the newsstand, himself a Marseilles man, with his convict number tattooed under his armpit, I had to step to one side a little because I had lost sight of her: but Joan has gone into the cinema, after all, has looked at the posters of the film that is forbidden to minors, the actress's breast grasped by a man's hands, and she has bought a ticket, coming in behind a group of sailors.

She was absorbed, too alone in those astonished stalls, the usherette came along and told her to put out her cigarette, and at the exit she says to me: I didn't believe that here in Marseilles: she was perturbed, excited like a girl at her first big dance, so we went back up the avenue until we reached the crossroads where you turn off for the hotel, the wind sent waste paper curling along the pavement, Marcel is following us, trailing along, perhaps right back to the room where he will spy on us through the keyhole, it was almost cold, Joan went into the bathroom and turned on the tap for a bath, there is a strange smell in the air as I close the shutters, the cathedral lit up, the high bastions of Fort Ganteaume, the white kepis that mount guard there, and now anything can happen, bugs in the mattress apart, I told her: never lift the carpets, they are thick with cockroaches, but Joan has got into the bath, a huge bath in the old style with brass taps, blue tiles, the mirrors already steaming up, my electric razor was there on the washstand shelf beside her bottles of cologne, and now I see my father's shaving brush, like a phallic symbol, quite dry and powdered with soap, his Mediterranean razor, the murderous blade, violence as a calling which is taking shape here and comes from far away, from his headlong lust which I sense in my own veins, we are no longer at Marseilles, but together in the bedroom in Viale Piave, and I shall be bolder than he, I shall dare what he could not, because to him it seemed vile to lie with my mother in a bath, the lift has stopped at this floor, a woman's step comes along the corridor, knuckles rap on the door, Joan was calling to me in amusement, she has a white bandeau across forehead and hair, I got into the bath with her, she says: why don't you read that book, she was still laughing when the maid came in, she sat on the edge of the bath and looked at us immersed in the water that was green from the bath-salts and edged with foam, this is why, I say to her, you have come all the way to Marseilles, this is what you want to try, my mother closed her eyes so as not to see, a fight seems to have broken out in the Algerian quarter behind the Head Post Office and the madly blaring horns of the police vans cross the night, however you do not understand how it can be she, the chambermaid with the little crown of lace, who is reading aloud, repeating in her own language those unnamable names, and suddenly every outside noise dies, barely the shaking of our bodies in the warm water, Joan too closes her eyes, savours the delight of a forbidden act, but the next day there is a monstrous grey moth resting on the edge of the bath, and Joan does not dare go near, get into the bath, because she is alone again, and Marcel's clothes were there, tossed on to a chair, and in the ribbed carpet over the floor there was a formidable cut that could have been made by a knife thrust.

I waited for her a long time in front of the newsstand where the night before we had bought that dirty book as a joke: and I don't know what happened between noon and four: we were coming back from the exhibition they had arranged at the Musée Cantini, 'Homage to Klee', which was really the story of Klee and the Mediterranean told in colours, little squares and rectangles of blue and green eyeing you from the surfaces of little paintings, and it was dawning on me that Joan's silence hid something I had not even suspected, sorry, she said, I must have been drunk.

I was persuading myself once more that I had her in my grasp, but an hour later when I was resting in the hotel and Joan had gone out to get the papers, there was the sharp crack of a revolver just below in Avenue Garibaldi, almost at the corner of the Canebière, I leapt to the window: a man in a raincoat, short, hatless, was standing half-hid inside a doorway, and Joan

74

came back a few minutes later as if nothing had happened, but from her breathing I could tell that she had run flat out for the hotel. And where are the papers? I asked her. There was no trace of Marcel either. If I had bared her back, I would have seen the selfsame reddish spots showing through on her immaculate skin now, the first signs of contagion.

'Hullo,' I repeated. 'Hullo.'

She was calling from the air-terminal at Marseilles, would I pick her up at the airport at nine, and other voices broke into the conversation.

'But who's that who's with you?'

'No one!' she shouted. 'Who on earth would it be?'

Then she added: 'Have you thought of me?'

I could not tell her how much of me she took away each time she left. It was Sunday, I had seen my daughter in the morning, and I was promising myself again that I would take up this book of mine which had not grown by a single page since our holiday at Portovenere. But I could not get started. If I tried to define the uneasiness that Joan's behaviour woke in me, I found it was like the feeling of being vaguely unwell, abstract at first, like the unusual sight of an object out of shape or out of place, the slightest of disfigurements that little by little brings anguish.

I turned on the radio, I thumbed through a book in an attempt to free myself from Joan. In the middle of the afternoon the street began to shine with rain, the image of Aldina, of the breast she offered me on the steps of her home, after a visit to the cinema, these

75

images super-imposed themselves on the others, en-larged to life size, without any obvious parallel.

Then, as present events develop, something is rent apart, your receiver goes dead just after the President has stressed the urgency of these measures. Joan would be here in a few hours. I repeated: fatal falls along the whole arc of the Alps, and on the rails across from us the train moved, but really we were in motion again, the smell of Aldina's skin, squeezing her waist in a third-class corridor, on our feet against the window and happy to be like that, bursting with desire at the beginning of our first holiday together, Aldina like my mother, and like her a dress-maker knowing nothing of Rome, two days in which we never even left the room we had rented from a shoe-making family in Trastevere: worn out by our tussles we devoured bananas, and Aldina threw the skins on top of the chest of drawers, from where a Virgin with a small light before her watched our spasms, Aldina's body was more ample, more baroque than any square or fountain we could have visited, never dreaming that she could be left alone, after we had ordered our bed-room from a furnisher's, or what your courage was when you reached her there under her dress to deceive her for a last time, her slender legs trembled, the train made us start pressed against each other, when the faces flashed by, aghast, behind the bars of a level-crossing: mum's giving us the fridge, and her hair was dishevelled in the wind of the train's speeding.

I could observe her hair quite closely, because the news was over, dance music was being transmitted, and Aldina was bent over me, the nape of her neck in close-up, offered to you, and you noticed the hairpins all awry with the passion of the act, her hair gathered on her head in a moving, overpowering wave, until you are no longer even sure this is her, but is perhaps Joan, a switching of parts that abruptly throws light on this act of veneration, on the hidden connections in it, but no, it is clear that it is Joan and Aldina has only been the first part of this fierce searching, this desire that lasts, that resists any wearing down, now you know you could not imagine Joan's neck bent over the same block as if awaiting the axe, without Aldina's help, and that even at the time when you sat with her on the couch in her home, by the light of the television, it was Joan you were looking for in the greediness of the other woman, in her shameless dedication, you were looking for a different fierceness, pride, say, the taste, the savour of combat which today is set before you, finally, as the sole condition for being alive.

There is nothing else, you were saying. And to Aldina, over and over: keep on, don't tire yourself, in the warmth of her mouth, and then in the scent of flesh you proved the world real, and the class struggle, the fire and the hell of it like an ancient curse, a bloody and necessary sacrifice to reach Joan, reach struggle in its final forms, of which you could know no more then than the cry Aldina stifled in the pillow. What would you have given to have her back, the loose and generous dress-maker, to bring you back that season of fury, of resistance, of certainties?

She says: the moon shone on the water as it does in summer, the sea looked a piece of tin-foil, but then from

Genoa onwards, clouds and rain.

So her absence this time, for two whole days, will end in the usual way: in a meteorological report, what the weather at Marseilles was like, and everything else be passed over in silence.

'You could have taken Marcel along with you. He's from Marseilles.'

'Of course,' she joked. 'The one thing I didn't think of.'

We were cruising along the straight road from the airport, lulled by the wipers, and brusquely, as we approached the tunnel, I swerved right towards the dim fields. I drew up at the first lay-by: the poorly-lit roadway, the black mirrors of the puddles could have alarmed her.

'Let's talk about things,' I said.

Then and there, she sought my lips. When we broke away, a veil of drops had gathered on the glass. I kept my forehead against hers, my eyes were losing themselves in two great lakes.

'Joan—but who are you?'

The two liquid circles seemed to widen. Now nothing mattered to me except sinking in them as soon as possible.

'My God,' whispered Joan. 'I can't believe this is happening.'

The display, the pomp of your ceremonies, the blue tassell on the sabre hilt at the Textiles Exhibition, the arrogant uniforms and the smell of brilliantine, the gleaming boots, those pig-at-the-trough faces parading with the emblems of power, the eagles of gold, the megaphone, a hated period of your Italy which lives on in these façades with the heavy sculpture, clusters of nymphs at Porta Magenta, you are walking carried along by your steps, without an apparent goal, but your instinct has already chosen the part of Milan where she lives, a very serious incident when a man is forty, as if going towards the only physical entity that joins us together, you skirt these buildings, their bare gardens, not yet aware of your need to call her up, from any kiosk at all, because the air is so clear that nature suggests the incredible is possible again: of feeling oneself in love, lightly but fully, walking at the level of a mystic ecstasy over the layer of dry leaves in the avenue, and not thoughts, sensations: a dog, the bench, some pure white paper in the waste-bin.

There was a tobacconist's with a phone right on the corner. I went in and rung her.

'Madam is resting,' replied the maid.

I asked her to wake her, just for a moment. Then her voice out of her sleepiness, trying to speak naturally.

'O nothing,' I explained. 'I just happened to be walking near your place.'

'Would you like to come up? Has something happened?'

Explaining was hard.

'Joan, I'm happy that you exist.'

A pause followed, I seemed to be drinking her breath through the receiver.

'Come. Come up,' she ordered, almost breathless.

'They haven't understood a thing about you, dearest. No one has ever understood one thing about you.'

A bus passing along the street shook the glass dish on which the pastries were laid. I myself was struggling to learn.

If we give voice to the unknowable, there is some hope of salvation: the paving tiles were white and black, lozenge-shaped, waxed, and they said nothing under the black man-style shoes of the Mother Superior, no echo to the rustling of the grey cloth habit, nor could I write of their missionary trainees who had come to occupy this villa in Via Paolo Uccello by simple chance, a small plaque on the door, the rusty bell-button which rang with a sound like school, this quiet, out of the way garden of torture in the San Siro district.

'The Sister with the keys is just coming. We never go there, down to the cellar.'

There were paper cut-outs of saints, fine pricked designs done by little Bantu boys or Polynesian girls, masterpieces done with bread crumbs by lifers, nativities scratched on the mother-of-pearl of shells, in a glass case in the corridor, and then those floor-tiles shining in the blaze of sun that pours down between the curtains, where heels have clicked, rough boots or riding boots, the arm held out in salute.

'But what are you saying?' the Mother Superior replied. 'Nobody calls it Sad-house any more.'

A song you learnt as a boy, perhaps because the interrogator's shout made the people living in the little villas around run to their windows. But what an idea, my editor had said, rake up those horrors, no one's interested in them now, but if it is a fact that the missionary trainees of the Immaculate are living there now, then, yes you could get a moving, a poetic article out of it, and that is why they have lifted up the cellar-flap at the end of the corridor, and the two Sisters and I are going down a winding stair in brickwork. The smaller of them lit the steps with an electric torch.

'Be careful, Sister Joan,' she warned the other who was behind me.

A staggering coincidence, as we lower ourselves down those few abrupt steps, as if we were working our way down a rock-face, and Sister Joan's soles are illuminated at moments by the ray from the torch which the other Sister shines back up at us, and her shoes are black calf lace-ups, well polished if cracked here and there, her white ankles hid in cotton stockings, and you feel grateful for the certainty they instil into you, that you must go no further, that here are neither knees nor thighs, but only those extremities shod in male shoes, a chaste descent like coming back down from Pizzo Stella with Joan, and I repeat to her: Be careful and don't slip, in the underground gloom that leads to the cells, I notice the iron-clad edge of the steps which broke the back of prisoners who were sent rolling down, kick after kick, it is right that these gentle warders should watch over their memory, and now I have to ask them:

'Is it true that it was the Cardinal who had the villa closed?'

'I wasn't here then, ask Sister Joan about it.'

She shakes the bolt at the door of a cell, gropes for a switch, Sister Joan tells me that she was not about at that time either, but the Mother Superior says that it was none other than his Eminence who wrote to

Mussolini so that this shame might be brought to an end, she pushes a little door wide and we are deluged in the light from the cell's four corners, blinding lights set into the wall and protected by wire-netting, no chance of breaking them, and I study the small blue tiles of the wall, looking for some trace, a scratched message, but it is not here that blood spurted, it was on the ground floor where the Mother Superior now has her office, the two Sisters stand to one side, and in the powerful light they watch me without speaking, look, Joan, when Auschwitz is a football pitch, no one will believe in these horrors, cigarettes stubbed out on open wounds, nails torn out with pincers, our city devastated by silence, and then, terribly loud, the howl of the tortured man.

'Can I see the other cells?'

Another and another, then another, all like the first one, only in this last there is a wrought-iron chair, what you find in a garden, this one was going rusty, Sister Joan explains that it was used for, and does not dare go on, that, in short, they tied the prisoners to it while they questioned them, and all three of us look on it with terror, this chair that does not talk, a skeleton, a fossil, a relic of greatness for those who could hold out and not tell a comrade's name, and I asked myself, if I would have resisted, now that Joan is my only greatness, biting the collar of my jacket till I fainted.

A murmur at my back roused me: the Sisters stood with hands joined, chin on breast, saying over a prayer. I did not dare ask any other questions, I did not wonder what I would write about this for the paper later on. I stared at the door, the little convent grating cut out

82

of the wood, the bars painted green, the joins in the planking, and you are in the queue at the public showers, in the foul-smelling steam, and little enough has changed since Cyklon B came out from the nozzles, the ceiling running with drops, the attendant pushes a brush along the floor, wet sawdust from which a cockroach rolls, and the numbers on the doors where the hot water dashes are so many cells like this one, death cells again, the tiles thick with grease in the Barcellona tube, a time that has not died yet, and they oppress us with brass instruments, ostrich feathers, goldfish, a mosaic of roses, and we are up to the neck in this, Joan, their lasciviousness is ours and the torture goes on, only hoping to find ourselves on the just side, with the tortured, and the one you are looking for is still her, the girl with the permanent wave and the cork-heeled shoes, loose as no other woman is, there is something repellent in those unshaven armpits, in those sharp knees, the very image of lust accomplished amid the firing, she who laughs as she bends back beneath a man, my Italy, though talking is in vain, hands that rub the self-igniting gun-cotton upon the bicycle bar, you, brunette of Monforte, who were waiting for the bus where the conspirator is journeying with false papers, and, arriving in Piazzale Baracca he will have to jump from the speeding tram while the gendarmes open fire and he falls heavily to the pavement in a pool of blood, where there is now an inscribed stone.

'Thank you, Sister, we can go now.'

There are no inscribed stones in the private road of Via Paolo Uccello. It was dark. On the surrounding wall, at the side near Via Masaccio, an inscription in whitewash sang the praises of the latest comrade, brought down a few days earlier by a burst of firing in the forest of Vallegrande, in Bolivia.

'What do you mean, you're not ready?'

At the paper I had got them to give me free theatre seats, the show was beginning in twenty minutes, and Joan was in her slip and no more, busy making up.

'I'll slip on a dress and I'm ready.'

But no, at the last minute she wanted another shade of stocking. Her wardrobe, with the door set wide, is a sight: the drawers spilling lingerie, the magnificence of her evening dresses, gloves, bags piled high. I followed her ready to catch her in flight as she came and went from the bathroom, and she informed me that she had dismissed her maid and would not want one from now on.

A stocking hung off the back of the chair, Joan was in the bathroom again. I went up to the mirror and began to draw the stocking over my head: sheathed like that, a face looks deformed, flattened out by the clinging mesh, the eyes are slits, the nose, pressed back, the lips are distorted by the silk transparency.

'Hands up,' I ordered from the doorway.

I thought that she did give a shudder at least: I frightened myself.

'Darling, not that, you look a monster.'

I caught her by the shoulders.

'Where's the safe?' I asked threateningly.

I tightened my arms around her, we fell down,

clasped together, on the bed, I saw the nape of her neck as in a film dissolve, Joan, pinned down by my weight, tried to free herself, shaking with laughter like a child.

'Ah, then I don't frighten you?'

'Go away, monster.' She was choking with laughter.

'Where's the safe?' I murmured.

So I had to unsettle her, with a violence I did not believe I was capable of, tearing the silken mask from my face to seek her mouth, until I quenched that laugh in her throat, until we both lay, a little while after, flat out, half-dressed, panting.

'Darling, what got into you?'

I did not know, and I did not care to know: a whim exploding, a new turn to the game, a need to possess Joan the moment she is ready and perfect, Joan as a girl coming out of the Ursulines' school, pretending not to see the chauffeur who waits on the pavement for her, a gesture, in short, that we will not regret.

'See what a mess you've made of me.'

The show had gone up in smoke, but there was a place I knew, an eating house where Sergino sang every so often for his friends. Joan changed, and finally we went out. It was cold outside, and on the road to Pavia, that follows the canal of the Naviglio, the cars roared by on mysterious expeditions. I thought that somehow ours was doing that, too.

'Let's hope that Sergino's there. He's a real character, you'll see.'

But on this particular evening he had not shown up yet.

'"Madam's" going about,' the proprietress quietly informed me. 'Dirty weather.'

Joan did not understand, and anyway it was best not to make her worry. We sat at a table in the private half, where youths were playing poker and a fair-haired lad plucked at a guitar. It was the usual dismal place, half eating-house, half bar, but with no billiard tables, with juke-boxes, and these youths who dashed out importantly and came back later to dine off a chop.

'We can go somewhere else if you like.'

'No,' she said. 'I'm enjoying myself.'

We passed comments on the faces that appeared and vanished, and I told Joan that, years earlier, when they had stolen my car from right under my window, it had been Sergino who had traced it for me, simply by asking questions in those circles. Sergino had chalked up nine years in the prison of San Vittore, and while he was there, he had become famous as the 'prisoners' lawyer', and in the recreation hours, allowed four times a day, someone would always come up to him to ask for legal advice, in exchange for a packet of cigarettes.

'Look,' I said. 'That's his girl friend.'

I waved to Rita who had just come in with her platinum hair, and she came over and sat with us. I did the introducing. Joan asked:

'What about Sergino?'

'It's strange he hasn't come,' she said. 'He's waiting for me here every evening, when I've finished.'

She meant her work which was finding clients in the bars of Porta Ticinese. And she laughed aloud at every quip of the youngsters who came into the bar.

Two queens came in as well, with bags and gaudy dresses, they waved to Rita, Joan invited them to sit down at our table, another bottle arrived with more glasses, and just then Sergino made his appearance with the collar of his jacket turned up.

'Sorry,' he said to us, 'but we should be getting along.'

We had to beg him to stay. With his huge chest swelling, he sang the catches and ballads he had learnt in San Vittore, where they are three to a cell and in summer this means that the water in the jug gets hot, the bucket stinks, the tar melts with the blazing heat, the bugs just fall off the ceiling, down on to the bed-clothes. Sergino sings falsetto, the veins on his neck standing out with exertion, of that picaresque and no-class world which my father always shunned, which he had seen and suffered in his deep South, but which I sought out from time to time to try and understand the springs of my actions and of his.

'Grand, Sergino. Grand,' Joan applauded.

Sergino spun round, the youth who was cradling the guitar stopped in mid-chord: two men in dark clothes, their hats still on their heads, stood motionless in the middle of the room, looking over the frequenters one by one.

'Sergino, don't let on,' Rita whispered.

'Papers, please,' the inspector gave the order out loud.

There was a door behind us which opened on to the courtyard, one of the queens made for this, but the arm of a plain-clothes man stopped him at the threshold. Sergino had brought out his licence, he sat unperturbed and a little proud of himself, opposite Rita, we all stood up, Rita explained: I'm with these gentlemen, and I looked out my journalist's card from my wallet, the blue light of the police-car goes flash,

flash, on the window, and there must be the van of the vice squad there too, parked near and ready to take on its load, they begin with the queens, uniformed police arrive now, and they have to push the two of them out.

'This isn't the season for coming to places like this,' the inspector said to me, as he gave me back my card.

In the other room the 4-2-1 was starting, as Sergino puts it, men with a record refusing to let the arm of the law drag them from their chops, then came the report of a slap, unleashed close in.

I turned to reassure Joan: she had gone.

'But where did she go?'

'The lady?' Sergino whispered. 'She beat it, first thing, soon as they came in, didn't you see her?'

All that was left of her, in that turmoil, was a lip-stick trace upon the rim of a glass.

I know that you lay there unmoving, not exchanging a word, in the afternoon heat, the silence marked by the twittering of the radio, German armour has broken through at dawn, in a thrust towards Leningrad, the very place that he with the black and white shoes calls Saint Petersburg, pockets of resistance are being mopped up, the number of prisoners, enormous, and with the first shootings, my father remembering that other silence in Viale Piave, that was quite identical to this one, at the first shootings, he saw her, my mother, running along, hugging the wall in the Porta Tosa quarter, two bullets smashed the windows of the room, Hungarian grenadiers were spread out in a line along the walls opposite, with their rifles up at their cheeks: without warning, axes are hacking, blow upon blow, at the door: fierce shouting: inside the house, a wailing: the innocent tenants, unarmed, caught up among running women and children, no other way out except across the roofs, the grenadiers on the roof and the military police in the street, have to stop that girl who is getting away there, holding up her skirts, but the soldiers are already on the landing, the axe fetches great gashes in the door, and then once in the rooms, they stab family portraits with bayonets and swords, kick in wardrobes, snatch up money, watches, silver, all Milan delivered over to looting, and a barricade is already up in the Passione quarter, but a low one, four or five doors and hand-carts, which the Hussars amuse themselves in jumping, because not one of the leaders has thought of it, of instructing them to barricade the fifteen bridges on the inner Naviglio, so my mother stopped for breath in a doorway only a hundred yards away from the family shop, a furnisher's, and a patrol of Croats comes along, dragging a young man with them towards the castle, she hears him shouting to the deserted street for help, fighting desperately with fist and feet, until his escort strangle him and hang him from a street-lamp, the officers laughing with gold epaulettes on their white jackets, the dark is coming down and it is beginning to rain this evening of the 18th of March on which my mother waits there without daring to look out from the doorway, because a Hussar has ridden against Micio (the one who stays at number twelve, Fontana district) and sent his perfectly good eye flying from its socket with a sabre-cut, but where are the leaders of the revolt? and who are they? meanwhile we have run to our bells, the ringing of bronze begins, calling from one bell-tower to another, they'll slit our throats on our own doorsteps, it makes no difference, if it is true that two battalions of Tyrolese from Crema are already in the outskirts, and one of Gyulai's from Pavia, just let the count tell us what to do, since the confusion is great, the fires of the bivouacs at night, round about the castle, a rumbling of carriages over the paving, the iron rims of the wheels, six batteries to defend Porta Tosa, and from the mound which rises just beyond, they call to her, my mother, these are her sisters calling, who are ready to throw down mattresses and benches down into the street, Milan is fighting, anyone with a weapon makes ready to move, when she broke from the doorway, in a short run, where the Palace of Justice now is, her heart throbbing in her bodice, perhaps counting on Manara who should be at the gate already, to start the fire, while she runs, her face twisted with the Lombard fury, she ran on pursued by shots in the darkness, to meet history, advancing from the South to take her, with bony Arab arms, on the couch of a rented room in Viale Piave.

'But where did you run off to?'

'I went home. Come over right away and I'll explain?'

'There's nothing to explain, Joan. Now I know you're mad for sure, and that suffices. There's no other explanation.'

I put the receiver down, began undressing, but I

could not exorcise the spectre of doubt which brought up one stupid reason after another that might have driven Joan to that meaningless escape: was it fear of the Law, a secret she could not admit to, but which the police could read in her papers, or was what was written there simply some hint of her being a suspect person, at this point I had to consider if Joan was her real name and not the one she had chosen to be known by at a critical turn in her life, and now I remembered that I had never opened her passport on any of the many journeys we had taken together; and if madness it was, I found myself thinking, there's method in it.

I looked at my watch: it was after two. I saw Joan lying in her large bed, then I came in and gave her a few good slaps, and the more closely I pictured this scene that could well happen, the greater was my desire to enact it: I would have forced her to admit the truth, to reveal her identity to me, at last, the woman I was in love with, who said 'in love with', I could say now, I had never been jealous of her; about her past I asked nothing, and she asked nothing about mine, and now this cancer, this aberration among the most common, that was the privilege of the many now, was dragging me along as I listed the most obvious possibilities: of Joan raped by someone, known to her or not, or, worse, her making wild love to one of those café-haunting youths, or, worse still, the willing spectator of a couple making love, or one of the participants in a private initiation ceremony, so you see that this is the most humiliating way to stimulate yourself, through a jealousy that wrongs both of you, but which the way of the world sanctions as holy and lawful, like the evening you waited for Aldina a whole hour, in front of her place, and to punish her, took and enjoyed her standing up on the steps that led to her home. You were not going to fall as low as that again, to the level of a drug-seducer: six ounces of sulphur, one of arsenic, six of Palestine incense, five grains of myrrh, five grains of mastic, mixed together and ground in a mortar . . .

I closed the book with a snap. On my work table, among the papers, lay an invitation from a club in Florence, to speak on Africa. I slipped into bed, lit a last cigarette: from the radio cabin, I saw the quiet stretch of sea, I was coming back from a job in Sardinia, the outline of the Ligurian coast beginning to show on the horizon, and I heard the signal that told me the line to her receiver was free, Joan was still living with her husband, I saw the bedroom of a married woman, as I imagined it, her pillow by his with a hollow in it where his head had lain, I felt a sudden tightening in the pit of my stomach, and then, almost immediately, the voice of a sleepy Joan, the radio operator had risen from his seat so I could speak at my ease, and her voice came over to reassure me: don't worry, he didn't bother me last night.

Beautiful, virile jealousy that speeds trains on their way, coming back from a journey, finding it impossible to sit down with a book, going up and down the corridors uneasily, observing with grim satisfaction the carcasses in the motor-car cemeteries, and even the heaps of dirty table-cloths and napkins in the restaurant car, the polished surfaces of the trays like hospital articles, the cold surgical violence of the screws, an unmistakable smell of gas containers, the smell of death by jealousy, and again, coming back by sleeper from

Warsaw, the fir trees whitening to the horizon, frost flowers on the window, the white of snow unmarked except for the fences, and rows of canes, a wooden roof here and there, lying back as if you were in a hospital train, being brought back from a battle that never was, an unformed design which only where the rails curved seemed complete to my eye, I raised chest and head from time to time, a line that was less white was probably a road, I lay back again, said goodbye to knowing, content to be questioning the shapes of clouds, the see-sawing of the telegraph wires, the shooting images of a cardiogram, went back to brooding on my wound, since Joan had dared *not* to turn up at our first appointment.

No, I had to avoid repeating these mistakes once and for all.

I put out the bedside lamp. The trip to Mount Stella, the outing to Sabbioneta, all the hours I had spent with Joan in that most carefree time of our story, already made up a season that was not to be repeated, now that unanswerable questions, each one harder than the last, struck home, vanished into thin air, came back to daunt me.

A rotating wheel of arms, of colours and noises, the sounds all mixed—my wild imaginings about Joan were like that, because I had also gone above eighty decibels of intensity, and yet it was bliss to stay with her at the point we had reached, that day on the Ile du Levant, going along the path, in the sun, that led between the rocks to the nudist camp.

Her fabulous hips shake at every step, a motion full of joy, the wood of seaside pines, the pervading scent of the resin, when we stop for breath, the sea beneath us too blue if anything, her skinny girl's body stripped naked, it had been her idea to come here, an hour and a half's trip by boat from Lavandou, I had spoken about it, yes, but as a joke and yet here she is walking along fast, not embarrassed to be showing all her shapeliness, but not proud to be, either, it seems natural, a game, to greet anyone passing, what does it do to you, I kept asking, nothing: the sea glittering, the bay, the little sandy beach for bathing, and other bathers on the rocks, scattered about like seals, as naked to the sun as we were, passing the notice which warns: 'adopt the ways of the naturist and you will be welcome', so now even the little strip of coloured cloth has to go, the g-string bought at the stall back there for a franc.

'But isn't there a policeman here, or a manager, or just somebody in charge?'

'I don't know, Joan, if there is, he's naked.'

We had laughed then, in the wind that brought the scents of rock and pine from near at hand now, I told her that the nudists always give a warning to any newcomer who has not taken off his last garment by burning his skin with the sun's rays reflected in a little mirror, I myself pull one end of the strip knotted about her hips, and Joan shows herself to all as she would show herself only to me, now we go into the wood, there are couples among the bushes, seated on the grass, slackly embracing, old men on their sticks, mothers knitting, I said to her: are you sure you don't want to turn back? and Joan drags me along by the hand, down the slope leading to the beach, into the Dante circle of bodies that are overpoweringly near, motionless in the sun, they are shooting a film, it must be the Odyssey, I thought, and I was struck just then by her indifference to it all, how naturally she opened a passage for herself, in that babel of all the crafts and languages, with an instinct so different from mine that she could feel we were hundreds of miles away, as we dive and break the water with mighty strokes, and then dripping as we clamber over those naked bodies and fall on our faces to dry in hot sand.

'Isn't it an extraordinary feeling?'

'Yes, it is,' I agreed.

Bathing so freely, with the feel of the sun on all your flesh, it was a new, a natural blessedness.

'Now I would like to make love—would you?'

'With all these people around?'

'As far as I'm concerned, they're not there.'

I had known the island ever since I had written a series of articles on it for an evening paper, but with Joan beside me I ended by feeling a casual tourist, just glad and no more to have beaten a taboo, inside the sunburnt hide of the old man you still are, the idea of nakedness is tied to the idea of pleasure, the excitement in feeling up Aldina in a wood, at twilight, with the taste of stealing in it, the vice of slowly baring her flesh, seeing that Joan has turned on her back now, a shell-fish peeled and open, now, to the sun and any glance at all.

I knew I was wrong, but what I feared was something quite different, and we spoke about it on the boat, and then again on our return journey from the Riviera, as of something indecent almost: my fear was that I might belong, without hope of redemption, to another age, one founded on average vileness: it had been the fear of losing Joan to the brute self in me, the fear of a satiety that, with others, had always come.

'Please,' I said to her. 'I can't bear it when you cry.'

Aldina had not even taken her overcoat off. Sitting on the bed, she had listened to all my explanations without saying a word. For my part, I had kept my raincoat on, the lamp gave out a dim light, there was a screen placed at the exact point where it had stood on other occasions, a dark veil to hide the foot-bath, I saw her slender calves, the crossed legs, the skirt raised by the posture, I know her whole body down to its last crease, it was as if I were seeing her naked that moment, and my indifference was confirmed.

'I don't believe it, it can't be true,' she said in the faintest of voices.

She stretches out a hand which I have to take, she draws me close, her eyes shine, her lips seek me.

'You'll get over her, you wait and see.'

'No, Aldina. I'm sure I won't.'

She it is who kisses me, who makes me fall with her, on top of her, so we are lying back on the pillows.

'We should be getting married in a month's time.'

'I can't go through with it, I've told you.'

'Is she prettier than me?'

'What does that matter?'

'What's her name? Do I know her?'

She holds me crushed against her breasts, as if I

were the one who needed protecting.

This room we call ours: the tinny ashtray on the bedside table, the worn hand towels ready on the washbasin edge, the mirror, the chiaroscuro which is swallowing us up along with these objects that I am getting ready to bid goodbye to.

'Aldina, not that, don't do that.'

She had unbuttoned her cardigan under her coat, and my face was now pressed in the hollow between her breasts, made deeper by the brassière.

'Be good, dearest. Just be good and stay there.'

Now the voice too has a certainty about it, perhaps I shall manage to tell her the most difficult part: that I am tired even of her body, that I have made a terrible mistake: will she forgive me for having desired her so much?

'Come on,' I say to her. 'Have a cigarette.'

I free myself from her embrace, Aldina refuses the cigarette, she keeps her eyes on me but does not listen, it is as if she were hypnotised, stretched out on the bed, her red overcoat wide open, she would certainly be desirable to any man coming in this minute, and I hear with irritation the delicate crackling of the silk as she moves her legs over the coverlet, without removing her shoes, and she pretends to listen, her mouth a little open, her breath coming short, as it does when she is excited, it's all over, Aldina, try and understand, how?—I'll have to tell you, I love another woman, but it is not only that, and I see her bosom heave as her breathing grows laboured, a naked breast peeping from the cardigan.

'You know, just yesterday,' she speaks at last, 'I went to see about those photographs.'

It was you who pressed her into doing it, after all, becoming a model for a stocking firm, the illusion of detaching her from you, of giving her new enthusiasms.

'I know, Aldina. You've already told me.'

'The photographer made me get up on a table. He says that he has to take my legs alone.'

She laughs, her eyes still wet with tears, and you should take hold of her and slap her this minute, stop her from going on with this self-abasement.

'How funny—it excited me.'

A silence followed, Aldina looked like a great covered fish, with something unclean, something I knew so well, about her whole body.

'And you . . . were you in your slip?'

She had lifted her skirt to the top of her stockings, to the band of flesh that shone out as it used to do, for just a second, clear and smooth and remote, she goes on to explain that, next thing, they put two powerful lamps at her sides to light up the scene, and they gave off such heat, and she was in her underclothes, standing up the whole time, holding her slip up and squeezing her thighs together, now she demonstrates what she did, she herself has turned the lamp round, it was enough just to touch her for everything to become confused, lose shape, come alive nowhere else but in that fire that Aldina gave herself up to, in her desperation.

Then we stood up, shattered, without saying a word. The bed creaked unbearably as, with mechanical gestures, you tied your shoes, a great void inside you as if you were in the presence of disaster.

'You do love me a little still, don't you?'

Her eye was blackened where the mascara had run.

'You can't leave me, can you? No other woman gives you just this, does she?'

I nodded in agreement, but I was weeping, for her too, the humiliated one.

I stretched an arm towards the phone, groping for it in the dark.

'The sun's shining,' said Joan. 'Good morning.'

It was almost nine, I had not even heard the alarm.

'Still angry with me? You said I'm crazy last night.'

'That's the plain truth, Joan. I haven't met another woman like you. I wonder if one exists.'

'I know, you haven't been so lucky.'

'What do you mean?'

'Nothing but ordinary women, all your life. You deserved better.'

'All right,' I yielded. 'I'll try inviting you to the theatre again.'

'What happened to Sergino?'

'They picked him up, but he'll wriggle out of it.'

'Can't you do something to help him?'

'I could do something for you.'

'And what would that be?'

I found myself suddenly desiring her, for a reason that I strained to understand, and perhaps it was just because of this everlasting whim of hers to test herself, to expose herself, to run away.

'Are you in bed too?'

'Now, I'm just about ready.'

She agreed to undress, something we had done over the phone before, love-making in the conditional sense,

'What I would do,' 'what you would do,' the thing conjugated furiously, impatiently, because of her antagonism, her aggressive certainty.

'And now?' Joan asked again.

'Now turn round,' I ordered. 'Like that: let yourself be seen.'

It is necessary to pay great attention to embers, which can remain live for a long time, they must be covered over with earth, and similarly all papers must be buried, as also tin-cans, and any food remains. It is essential to observe the strictest silence when the column is on the march: to prevent fires being lit in open places, or any column of smoke rising before nightfall.

'Darling, I can't go on with it,' Joan murmured into the receiver.

Then, once you have ascertained where sentries are posted, what the lay-out of the barracks is, and how many men are there to defend it, you work out the actual plan of attack, always remembering that it is better to launch a frontal attack by night rather than in daylight, when the enemy has greater ease in bringing up reinforcements.

'Joan, get into your car and come right over here.'

She said she could not, that they expected her at her shop, but, more important, that I should not be late at the paper.

'None of that matters a damn to me, come over here.'

'Better if I don't.'

'Joan, why aren't you here this moment?'

I could sense the perfume and the delight of her skin, drink her breath from the receiver. It was at that point that my voice said:

'Joan, we've got to live together.'

It was cold outside, an anti-cyclone from the Azores, hanging over this spring day in Via Manzoni, a new government crisis was out on the stalls, and you have parked your car far away from the hotel. It was Joan who had taught you never to leave it nearby; during our clandestine meetings. You went into a pastry shop to choose cakes: this, too, was a rite, in my daughter's name, and then into a telephone kiosk to make sure that she had got home before her husband, that everything was oh, perfect in the comedy we had forced on ourselves.

There, on the other side of the door, the child shrieking, a little voice to hold to, in moments of doubt. She will grow up, you said, one day she might understand even this: how you stood on the mat and waited for the door to open like a theatre curtain on Act Two, noticing how the wound closed again each time, and the split healed that meant a daily agony, or worse: a habit, a mechanical playing over of set words and gestures. How you stand just now with wrapped cakes in your hand and the scent of Joan on your body.

'Oh,' she says, 'you've brought the cakes.'

This woman, who feels no need to pretend she is alive, to lie.

'Did you listen to the news?'

'No. Why?'

'The government has fallen. Switch the set on.'

'All right,' she says. 'You'll be happy.'

She opens the paper round the cakes puts flowers in

a vase, and the vase on a table that is laid ready.

'But can't you hear how bad this child's cough is?'

Joan, crouched up against the headboard of the bed, looks straight in front of her, one strap of her chemise off her shoulder. Was this really your battle?

Domestic cowardice is also the wine in the glasses, the flickering television screen, the well-brushed clothes in the wardrobe, or better: the sure judgement, the lace collar that spreads out broad on the chests of Flemish burgomasters, while you slacken your tie and sing: Up then and fight, our Ideal at last will be . . . dear Lombard autumn that evaporates on the glass of french-windows, the petunias are already wrapped in cello-phane out on the terrace, I remember we got up from table, and you are on the divan, the Swedish divan, and you open the paper, the evening paper, and you lose yourself in the rioting at Jakarta, you find you are having to go back and read again, meanwhile on the small screen the bombers' targets explode silently, a presentiment that all this will go on and on, and let it be just like this: that you idly cross one leg over the other, shod in handsome moccasins, and the little Viet-cong slithers about barefoot in the paddy—this would be the least of it, it has happened before—when sud-denly among the images that succeed one another and the well-inked words, a crack opens, a small gap at first, but something has happened. No more than a suspicion, the shade of a doubt, and, of course, you have a company behind you with its capital fully paid up and the whisky bottle comfortingly near: the doubt that your day would be different and richer with Joan.

'Couldn't you talk to me sometimes, me too?'

You went back to your reading. Someone you do not know is waving from the top of aeroplane steps, not one object changed, the windows misted with autumn silence, the vase of philodendron swallowed up in eternity, just like us. She is sitting opposite you on the divan, you could tell her straight off that this living together does not make sense any more, that the boredom that is crushing us, springs from nothing else, the emptiness once filled by our love-making right here, by the opalescent light of the small screen, where she became pregnant.

'Either you don't talk or you are away on your travels!'

'What do you expect?'

She shrugged, then rose up abruptly.

'We got on so well together,' she said against the glass of the french-windows, she draws back the curtain, stays there for a long, long time, and you only hope there are no tears. Neither of us dreamt how near we were to the end: a news bulletin filled the room with calm lies.

Like ash on a white suit. I blew and this uncertainty vanished, the doubts, the questionings. Specially if Joan looks at me as she is doing now, standing on the platform with the other people saying goodbye.

'Leave me, dearest, you'll be late at the shop.'

She hardly bats an eyelid, smiling there, and I want to carry her off with me, this moment, on this train.

103

'You staying in Milan?' I asked now.

'I think so. When do you get back from Geneva?'
The carriage lurched into motion.

'Remember what I told you.'

She nodded gravely, gathered her fur-coat up at her cheeks, then suddenly called out:

'Think of me a little, if you find time.'

I just touched her fingers stretched towards the window. I was sure of doing a solid piece of work in the two days I was to have at Geneva whether the Person was there or not, and anyway I felt I could have invented a superb interview, free as I was now of every nagging thought, and determined not to succumb to them again.

It was raining on the Lago Maggiore. I thought my thoughts, as if they were already printed, a state of grace that came to me from Joan, from the promised life that I was perfecting in mind. At Domodossola as we waited for the customs men, it snowed thickly and the flakes came fluttering down from the arc lamps, a youthful couple on the stationary train next to ours kissed brazenly, she was resting her head on the window and his arm lay on her shoulder so that his hand coming under her chin forced her to turn towards him and meet mouth to mouth, I saw the sticking plaster that he had on one finger and that easy way that foreigners have of kissing in public. First to come on was an official, an arm-band over his rain-coat sleeve, he spent a long time examining the pass-port of the man opposite me who bent over his daily *Spiegel*, and the bulge on his jacket front was something unbelievable, just under his breast pocket, it could have accommodated an automatic complete with silencer, a chloroform pad, perhaps even a syringe filled with drug solution, a game, this, to distract me from the only words I said over in myself for Joan alone, a few lights in the gloomy depths of the valley, the snow which was becoming big drops, I sat there mentally composing, letter by letter, statements that had already occurred to me, also because at Brigue 'when train is standing in the station', it does not do to go out and urinate on the platform, then a skating-rink, lit up and deserted in the snow, like an apparition that is significant but who knows why, and the fulness of being which swells you, for no reason, already makes this December night eternal.

I got down at the station of Lausanne to get cigarettes from a machine. The post office on the platform was still open, I went in by instinct, I should have told her that I was good for another forty years but that there would be no further repetitions, thanks to the intensity of life with her and my awareness of it, but in place of that, I filled the telegram-form with a few words, the girl assistant counted them one by one, then glanced up with amusement at this phrase from an Italian song.

The compartment was half empty now. I went out and smoked in the corridor, the lake was invisible, what could be seen was country, rough but thick with unquestionable signs, *ne pas se pencher au dehors* and strange warnings *Kein Trink wasser*, which only now you take in: the little cemetery in the snow, the sudden thump entering a tunnel, the fragility of a bridge as it is illuminated by train-windows flashing by, the great burst of an express going the other way, in short, excitement until you were sick with it, until the rails run close to the lakeside road lit up by tall street-lamps.

There were stretches in which we raced the powerful cars that hurtled along the straight roads, a few yards below us, and a welling up of happiness, the unnamable word, took me unawares, and there was no trace of Joan in it, but, if anything, the taste of liberty finally restored to me, as the rhythm of wheels on rails beats it out from time to time: the plane-tree on the road, a gate, a green rise even greener against the leaden sky, the old colours of the North that you can read in the darkness of Leman, familiar, perhaps the mistaken belief of being able to live to themselves, or even of being able to serve others better, and we would have to know if we have people who can make Molotov cocktails or construct a time-bomb, because the materials could be found here in this country where with their precision they can split the second, a problem that is already in the past, according to some, if it is true that the people in the streets would take the initiative when the opposing forces met, flags and slogans carried in processions, the smart regiments that mutinied at Petrograd, what a lovely dream for us to be at the Smolny Institute, but no, we are all of us drowning in 'the way to phrase the problem': it is probably because of this that the thick steel plate of the railways of the Swiss Confederation is so deeply satisfying, and the odour of this mist with the highest percentage of suicides, Drink Greatness as you look out in the wind, as you go up to the firing line, but there is something more: the café where Lenin, the villa where Bakunin, unchanged the colour of the lake, unchanged the dull struggle against the system, that is, ours is the obsolete system now, even Mazzini, his fingers dirty with printing ink, in the little typographist's at Geneva, digging the sand out from under your enemy, but indistinguishable from him on the same red carpets, in well-padded lifts, pillars of yesterday's world, of the world that is still Joan's.

But is it my fault she retorted at our first meetings, not to have been born in the porter's lodge?

And still you wonder if she ever had a purity, Joan, like the one you have lost, from the time when my father, in a third-class compartment, taught me to recognise the rivers of Italy, perhaps as he was eyeing the legs of some woman on a journey that seemed endless even to him, because he could not loosen his collar without declassing himself, my mother overcome by the heat in that dress covered with little poms, you stared at the hydrangeas on the platforms of wayside stations, but above all at the stage-sets of concrete in city suburbs, a whirlwind of tyres, corrugated roofs, washing thick as leaves, the peeling façades, the harsh territory of the railroad itself, then interludes of light on great open fields bare of grass and white-washed frames stuck there, goal-posts without a net, the youth of the world, from the time when you both took me by hand as soon as we got down at the tram terminus, with Italy that is going right forward, and then challenging me in the third declension, us like others at Novosibirsk or in New City, along a fence that smelt of fresh paint, proud to be left alone to fight it out.

Why not tell me that all that was nothing but illusion? You would have spared me the selfsame weaknesses, this desire to live a future that is different. But no, deluded by some greatness, by reason of the wind which, rushing in through the carriage window, stops the breath in your throat, you went on describing the objects of your nostalgia, obstinately setting store by her dress with the little white and blue poms, by her straw-hat with its ribbon, by that train with the fascist emblem, by the blackened window-frames themselves, half-shattered by the blast of passing expresses.

Geneva, the city of armistices, offered me chocolate with cream. The next morning I tried getting in touch with the Person direct from my hotel, but His Highness had had to leave abruptly, so I invited his secretary to lunch, and the driver tells me that there are easy chicks everywhere, even in this honest Confederation at whose edges the waves of Europe subside, and the taxi drew up alongside the terrace.

There were no swans on the lake, yet the little tables were lined up outside, the icy west wind flapped the edges of the cloths that covered them. At last a limousine stopped, a young woman got down, and my heart stood still: the width of a road separated me from Joan.

'Listen to this: the clearing away of leaves this autumn has cost the Council more than five million lire . . .'

'Joan, I asked you a question.'

She closed the paper, but did not put it down.

'Have you really thought about it? You know what it means?'

'I know that it is senseless to go on like this. I want us to live together, I'll come here, or you'll come to my place, or we'll look for somewhere else. But no more of this. No. I can't go on "seeing" you wherever I go. Because I know very well it could be you really, in any quarter of the globe, because I know nothing about you, or your mysterious journeys, your disappearances, nothing!'

She rose up to light a cigarette.

'It's a risk I can't take.'

'But why not?'

She inhaled, shook the match to extinguish it.

'You'd weary, everything would come to an end. Try and understand.'

'Joan. I thought of nothing else all the way back from this trip. It would be different, this time.'

'No, the mistake is built into the system. And the mistake is just that: a man and a woman's wanting to live together, you've always said so yourself.'

Her tone forbids any answer, the feeling is as if she were teaching me how to fly, how to get off the earth, rise away above the loudspeakers, above the materials of everyday reality, into an unexplored region that only she knows, where the past does not count and the present alone exists.

'You wouldn't send me any more wires from Lausanne telling me you love me: I'd be right in your way, day and night. Just try and imagine it.'

I had come back determined to provoke her, to shout aloud at her that the truth was oh, so different, that is to say, that this way suited her, keeping quiet about her private life, and here she was helping me, in spite of my intentions, to kick off my vileness and find I was still capable of something generous.

'You were so different from the others, and I fell in love. But I can stop, you know, if you prove a delusion.'

The telephone rang.

'What's more, for people like us, love is a kind of constant struggle.'

'Aren't you going to answer it?' I put in.

'Something we have to win day by day . . .' she went on.

I rose up abruptly, Joan rose up too, to stop me approaching the telephone.

'Stand aside.'

'Have you gone mad?'

The call rang on and on, perhaps Marcel, perhaps her husband, perhaps someone from Marseilles, in any case, a voice that was to remain a mystery, because suddenly the ringing stopped.

I had gripped Joan's wrist, now I let it go, her eyes were full of tears.

'Sorry, if I hurt you.'

'O, it's not that.' She spoke quickly, biting her lip.

'Well then, I'll see you tomorrow.'

'Of course.' Joan forced herself to smile.

I picked up the coat I had left over the armchair, Joan was leaning against the door-post, her arms crossed over her breast, defending everything about herself that I was never to know.

What the sense of all this may be, between expectation and fulfillment, and what the true price of this restless pursuit and catching something for a few moments only, which even as we hold it seems tainted, or at any rate not up to our expectations, and all around the daily words are raining down, in a sea of words

we drown, not all of them wanted for sure, and I, come
to Florence to speak about Africa, so now is the moment
when you can ask yourself these questions, as you put
chance remarks to those who have come to hear you,
a dance you cannot escape from, impossible to do figures
that are not in the book, you look over the audience
crowding the little hall, you speak and the more you
speak, the more tenuous and empty grows what you
meant to say at first, Africa that cannot be defined or
contained in a turn of phrase, described, classified by
impressions, and tables and truths and lies, in fact the
further you go, the less aware you are that you have
come into the truth, into the heart of what you really
meant to say, that is, to lay bare the intuition that
struck like lightning on one of the usual mornings—
but this time it is at the entrance to a cinema in Kow-
loon during the riots at Hong Kong, where they were
showing 'President Mao is a Red Sun for our Hearts',
the streets of the working-class quarter barricaded by
police with helmets and cane-shields—so many words
which we shipwreck in, printed or spoken, a sea of
words in which Joan, as with Joan not to be grasped
through adjectives, my personal mysterious Africa,
little jungle of traps and sweetest creeper.

I saw those faces in rows upon the seats, leaning
wearily or thrust forward, the black pits of the nostrils,
I should have let the howl of the Simba reach them,
shaken them with the blood of the rebels whose throats
were slit, instead they listened passively to the percent-
ages of literacy, and little by little Africa sunk from
sight, salesman of words, taking bits from every quarter
of the globe you can knock together a fair experience
of hotel usages, of ports of call and linking ships, but

you know less about man every day, you go round and round, and the centre of the world, for you, is still the street where you grew up, the house where we lived as children, the unbroken nut of childhood, the only restricted area I set against Joan (who did not know where I was today), like a declaration of war: childhood, my memories, a past stubbornly recalled so it could throw its light against the light from hers.

Look, she says to me. The snow carts were coming along from Piazzale Loreto towards Porta Venezia, Meneghin the joker and Cecca the gossip, their faces red in the wind, my mother lifted me every so often so I could see the carnival figures beyond the crowd's heads, deafening applause and laughter, in that February of 1935 on Corso Buenos Aires, and the booming of the big drum which I heard inside the fur collar of the coat that was a gift from Uncle Peter, my mother with her lean neck in the fox-fur sprinkled with carnival pellets, panting each time from the effort of raising me up, and he, my father, rose up from the bed and came over bare-footed to the window and looked down on the procession of floats, but did not see us, mixed as we were into the crush of people, nor did he imagine he was looking at the very thing that we watched, our hands numb with cold, he forgetting for a moment the female voice that calls him from the bed, rapt out of himself, he too, by this festivity in the street, and you have only to raise your eyes up to the windows of the hotel opposite where he came an hour ago to meet this woman whom even my mother knows, and now you can see him, with the same look he has when he is smouldering with rage, striking into her pelvis in the same way he did that Sunday in his young bachelor's room, only that a great silence came down afterwards, and he blew smoke towards the hanging light and the bowl of it is full of dead flies, anyway this adventure has been going on for a year now, but he himself has already explained to her that there is no way of resolving it, that the family is not to be touched, cannot be abandoned, and he swears to defend, with all his strength and, if needs be, his blood, the cause of the revolution as printed on his membership card.

Let that do, she says to me. Our breath shows clear on the dark sky, the tram-lines glitter when my mother once again puts me down on the pavement, she lingers in this icy air that makes her screw up her face, she puts off going home as if she were afraid she would have to wait for him too long, he who has gone back beside the woman under the blankets, to grapple, to wear himself out in a few spasms, because tomorrow, when the holiday of Sabato Grasso is over, because the whole world goes in the one boat and cock is rudder, as Uncle Peter says, tomorrow is Sunday.

Now, at least, you know what is left for you: this final mild heat, the sun of Brianza through the leaves in the trellis-walk, the patch of sunlight where your daughter pokes about with a little stick, the chalice on the stone table shines in its rubies, another Sunday at the Moulin de la Galette, and we are at the lake of Oggiono, in the din of the crowded tables and the

stench of fried fish, astounded by the clarity of this
water that is barely ruffled at all, by the ashen ridges
that they call the Pre-Alps, our seats set towards the
infinite, so we can talk more easily of trifles.

Out of all the certainties you could boast of, only
one bears you up; that of having Joan in your breast
like a wound, even if this other she (or just because of
this) is encouraging her daughter, and yours, with:

'Don't be afraid, the dog won't hurt you.'

She has come running back to shelter herself, her
little dress stained with mud. For an instant you sensed
with horror how conventional all this was, not exclud-
ing the perfection of her running up with the little
stick grasped in her hand, and you wonder how it
could ever amuse you, as it did once, to lose yourself
at one of the merry tables, with the country accents
of the furniture dealers, with dogs, grandmothers,
rubber boots, howling infants, the dusty black bottles
up from the cellar, tyre marks on the grass.

If you still came, it was to escape being alone on a
holiday, to try and deceive yourself into believing that
a man can resist, keep true, as our elders did, to a vow
of duplicity.

She stood up, went after the child to keep her away
from the lake's edge. She comes back to her seat, lights
a cigarette, we would have to go, she says, if we don't
want to be at the end of the queue on the way home,
and this is probably the moment to tell her all, that
you have been in love for four months now, that you
are up to the neck in it, this is the likeliest moment, in
short, for picking up this knife and stabbing her, from
inside her guard, while, eyes closed, she is breathing
in the light, as if she did not know what is there the

114

whole time behind our silences.

'If they don't send you away this week, you must come and do that little bit of shopping with me, don't forget.'

The sort of thing you used to enjoy, to be honest: picking the carpet for the child's room together, mixing with the crowds in the big stores, signing cheques like declarations of war, and then there's this piece of furniture we went to see in Valtellina, at an antique dealer's there, and where should it go exactly, because there are lots of things which can distract a man just at the moment when he is burning with desire to measure up to greatness: things above all, knick-knacks ardently pursued along half the market stalls of Europe, knowing in exact detail how a man dies in the paddy fields, and also fastening your top button carefully.

'Frank phoned. To give you his best wishes. And to say that you've gone right out of circulation. You never turn up at any of the gatherings now, he said.'

How clear the lake is: this prodigality of nature as she renews makes human ties less binding—to go where, if the humidity in those jungles where the guerillas fight would finish you off in no time, and even in one of our own prisons you would be abject as a dog—but even less tolerable was that one and only absence, Joan's.

'You choose,' I said, 'you're much better at it than I am.'

'It was so we could do something together. We don't even talk to one another now, haven't you noticed?'

It is like a steady drip, dripping, Sunday, the pauses, the answers, and you were already in the bar from which you call Joan every morning, a nondescript bar, recently opened in the neighbourhood where your paper has its office, a morning glittering with mirrors and bottles of Italian brandy, and on the mock-wood panelling hung a seascape that dated from my father's time, the waves breaking in spray right above the bar itself, now you know why you said 'Joan' in a discouraged tone, you were stifling the resentment in yourself for this ever more glaring complicity between you and him, brought together in a dismal story of adultery.

My daughter had run up to make me a present of wild flowers, I lifted her up and held her to me tightly. Keep calm, I told myself, but I was running away.

To go right away,' I said. 'Anywhere, but right away.'

Yvette listened to me, serious-faced, as she leant back on the pillow, her hands clasped round her knees, through the open window came the sun of Nairobi on that fresh January morning, traffic noises from Delamare Street, the klaxons of the tourist buses that were striped like zebras, I too had been on safari, come to that, had brought down Yvette at nineteen in her gold-buttoned uniform.

'That's just the reason why I chose this job, too: to go away.'

'Ours is no going, Yvette. We always come home. Really going away means breaking, walking out, cutting right through the old ties.'

It humiliated me to find myself one with him, to feel powerlessness exactly like my father's before the situation that had put my mother and me not a hundred yards from him, on that avenue, and now the Masai with woollen caps, right under us, walking about in front of the Stanley Hotel, waiting until we too give in and buy one of the bows and a feathered quiver, until I make up my mind to detach myself from a body that had taken me back, too easily, to the first blunt reasons for existing, only that here the window was set wide to the upland breeze, I saw in the distance the white fences of the race-course, and Yvette would be back at Orly before nightfall.

'Why don't you stop off at Paris too? I've got leave, we could spend a few days together.'

She had asked that of him, too, the woman who lay half-naked under the sheets in that room that was rented by the hour, as she shivered with cold, could they never have a whole afternoon to themselves.

'What about your boy friend?'

She shrugged, puckering her lips, we played for a little while, as we dressed, pretending it was all so possible, where would we dine in Paris, as if I did not have, I too, a job and obligations to honour.

'If I'm passing through Milan, I'll phone you.'

'Be sure you do, Yvette.'

She was in underclothes, wearing a blue slip and shoes, she looked like a girl out of *Playboy*.

'And by that time perhaps you won't remember Nairobi any more . . .'

It had not been easy work, pressing her to cross the threshold, of my room in the first instance, and then of her usual experiences, the essential thing had been to sweep her off her feet one way or another, communicate the same frenzy and the bewilderment to her, and it was he who came to my aid, from that bed where he lay on Corso Buenos Aires, my fingers were his, gentle and precise as his razor, and his, the persuasiveness on my tongue and lips, this art that is not learnt but carried in the blood, the power to throw yourself into what you are going to enact as a right and necessary gesture, that may perhaps not alter your life, but is not to be erased, although it was perhaps Joan you were thinking of at the beginning of that adventure, of Joan just met who resisted you quite effortlessly, just as Yvette had done for the first two hours as she danced with you in the hotel's own night-club, ashamed to admit that she had never let herself go right to the end.

So there was no call really to force things, but I had to prove that I was as good a head-hunter as he had been, that, much more than satisfying a whim: to come together again in this, the only real thing we can do, being Arabs like him, lecherous and prodigal, greedy for money but only so as to throw it about, like him polygamous and unfaithful in love, I had always mixed with them, in the Algerian quarter, I looked at white women the very same way that they did, I came rushing down the steps behind them to eye them, behind the plate-glass of a café, from the pavements of Boulevard Rochechouart, and in those glances you find the anxiety, the throbbing of veins, the cold, feverish anger of ripe desire, this is what fights in you opposed, as the phagocytes do inside our fibres, opposed by the industrious Lombard genius of my mother, with Viennese pronunciation, not *toder*, I say Viennese, a practising Catholic and blue-eyed, with the aristocratic dash of a waltz.

'Come here, Yvette.'

Not sated yet, still wanting to know, to feel out your story on her body: my Medina, the archways of the doors, the alleys and the twists, the swishing of fountains, the huge shadow of the woman mound, going deep into the casbah, headlong down the flights leading from the citadel, then climbing again to the slopes of the bosom, right inside the ears, in the crevasses revealed by frenzy, upright on the sky, the minaret of Nairobi, bend more Yvette because we are at the roads, shaking out the sails on the last corsair galley.

'*Viens, chéri*, or we'll miss the plane.'

There was a pointer, lying almost at my feet with its muzzle stretched towards the shooting-stands, under that high wooden shelter which smelt of cartridge smoke, and I watched the outlines of its bones which showed through at each breath, then Joan's head, slightly bent towards the shoulder, the gun raised and steady.

She had arranged to meet me at the shooting ground where she had come back just that morning to fire off a few shots with old friends. We had not seen one another since my talk at Florence, I would have liked it better if I could have been alone with her, but Joan must have realised that it would be easier to begin talking again, after the brusque interruption at her house that evening, if we were mixing with others.

She wore boots and a big leather jacket, it was misty at the horizon, and you could barely make out the lines of poplars away in the distance, like vague combs in the mistiness, Joan loaded in a hurry, I heard the click as the barrels snapped home, her high voice calling 'pool', the sweep, the bang, and the clay pigeon blasted a few feet above the ground. As I watched her, I felt sure that she missed more often than not, that, in the event, she was less infallible and inhuman than I might have been tempted to imagine, in some trepidation as she waited for the clay plate to come skimming out, I was one with it, describing the short trajectory at two hundred metres a second, I escaped the first shot but with the second Joan's pellets blew me to bits, so then I went back to seeking new paths of flight, mysterious tracks along which I could run and reach safety unharmed, and all the time I heard the echoing of shot upon shot as if her role were to punish.

She turned my way and signed for me to join her on the stand, but I did not want to measure myself against her in a contest that I knew I had already lost, I stroked the pointer's back, I stamped to keep warm, the cigarette smoke mixed with the steam of breathing, I was slumped down there among the few spectators, enjoying the gleaming of the barrels, the strong pungency of the gunpowder, the leather gun-cases, aware of everything that tied me to Joan, even the part of her world that at the beginning I had rejected: the slight acquaintances, the men of importance, the round of obligations from all which Joan had gradually detached herself, but which had been her world and her husband's before we met.

'I beat Franchetti, did you see? He missed four more than me.'

'Joan is as murderous as ever,' he said, shaking my hand.

'You let me try your automatic?' she asked Franchetti.

'Later on,' I said.

We sat on the bench, he told me he had read my article on Sad-house, this as a kindness to Joan, he even added that he had found it amusing, almost all Joan's friends were like that, you could not expect too much. We were joined by a young couple who had finished, Joan moved up close to me to make room for them, they talked indignantly of someone who had resigned, without mentioning his name which, however, must have been in the paper that day, and Joan murmured in my ear: 'An idiot.'

'I love you,' I said, gratefully.

She slipped an arm under mine, hugging up close to me like a student girl just out of her exams, Franchetti had lit his pipe, we ordered hot chocolate, I was almost merry, once again I was forgetting my doubts, drunk with all those shots from English guns, and I should have said so to her: that the tactical principle of conserving ammunition is fundamental in this type of warfare, and the firing must be methodical, sporadic, never wasting a round, and, if anything, fixing in advance the number to be used in the ambush, only Joan had slipped her fingers inside my sleeve, had undone the button at the wrist of my shirt so she could work her hand upwards more easily, blissfully I heard the shouts and the shots as I got down with her at that hotel, the porter set down the bag and opened the window which gave on to a swimming pool which was not part of the hotel itself but had been built for races, so in the morning we woke to pistol shots going off right under our window on the edge of the pool, I thought of a shooting ground, but it was the junior races, and so, after that first moment between sleeping and waking, we found ourselves making love to the starter's gun, in front of the youths who thrashed it out, cheered along by their relatives, it was somewhat embarrassing, even those rare swim-creatures named over the loud-speaker, with the figures and times obtained, all of it seemed to be addressed to us, grappled together there, and also to be timeless, belonging to another, an unmoving Italy, the one that had been yours, Olympic and Roman.

You were studying the face of the handsome prince beside her proud one, two hearts two dynasties two peoples spread right across the page, 'fairy-tale couple' they were to you, in the dampness of that flat at Porta Garibaldi that looks out on the railway, and she, my mother, with her belly five-months curved, has risen to clear the things away, noon in October 1929, and now he is reading aloud with his accent that just doubles the consonants, of how the young prince and princess escaped the dastardly attempt of that traitor, the exile De Rosa who missed with his revolver shot, from the position he had taken up on Rue Royal, while on the New York Stock Exchange something is happening that you do not even notice, a news item of a few lines from one of the agencies, and he asked my mother if she would like to be in the place of this Belgian princess, just as a joke, but he made her swing round, as she was putting the water flask back on top of the sideboard, to say oh no, it's enough when you love me, if you will always love me like this, and in fact you did not go to Piazzo Duomo next day to clap for the august fiançées, in the enthusiasm of flags and shouts of long live the Savoias, of flowers thrown from balconies on to the open car, of anthems for our native land and for the war, and already the materials of your greatness were being prepared, the white marble for the axe-and-bundle sign of the Fascists, the travertine tougher than bombs, your country like a big builder's yard, favoured with malaria and ideologies, of fresh bricks, of vocal greetings.

It was then, after he had sat her on his knee and stroked the belly where I was sheltered, it was on Thursday the 31st October that my father had the first suspicion that he had fallen into a trap he himself had laid, resolute as he was to keep his honour—not to be a rotter, he will shout one day in a fit of rage—only then that the truth was known about the black Saturday on Wall Street, but that afternoon Chrysanthemum Day was running its course, under the auspices of the Combat Groups, the 'Fasci' of Milan, and so he who had climbed up to the North as though it were a land to be plundered, come ashore from a Saracen vessel, a jotter full of adolescent verse, too, shut in the case that held his possessions, he could be well content with this, with her arms, too soft, too slender, that hung about his shoulders, as together they run over the insertions on the advertising pages, offers of employment, at this very moment, she says, when 'it' is about to be born, you have to find something, you have to find, he has risen up, has gone out on to the verandah, a biplane is flying low and you see the cockpit, the pilot's head, why, any sort of job, this is not how he had thought of starting out, unemployed a few months before becoming a father, because of a fall in shares thousands of miles away, even a position as a cashier, but how was he to know it was an American firm, and so now leaning on the verandah railing, staring out at the goods wagons in the marshalling yard, the petrol trucks in long, unmoving lines, he could wonder what fate lay in store for us.

'Do you see it?' Joan said. 'A grey car, look in the mirror, it's been following us for the last half-hour.'

I slowed down, and at once the car behind slackened speed, we were going along at seventy, with about nine miles to go, so in a few minutes we would have left the motorway.

'Who says they're following us?'

I accelerated: I wanted to be sure that Joan was not mistaken, but it was myself rather that I wanted to reassure. I suddenly gained a good hundred yards, but a few seconds later the yellow eye-sockets of those headlights were back again, stamping their glare on our mirror.

I looked at Joan: she was clearly alarmed, but what was worse, her uneasiness threatened to infect me.

'It's a foreign car!'

She said she had seen it when we were setting out, too, at the toll-barrier at Milan, it was two cars behind us, with three men in it, but she did not manage to read its number plate.

'Don't turn round, Joan, make as if nothing unusual's happening.'

I braked sharply, let them almost bump, then

abruptly accelerated.

'They'll be right up on us in a moment,' I said, and I was the troubled one as I raced flat out down the last five miles of motorway, because, no doubt about it now, they were following us.

'But why a foreign car?'

Joan was smoking in little nervous draws and had slipped down a little in the seat so that her head hardly protruded at all, as if she feared to be shot at from behind.

'Perhaps if you stop altogether . . .'

I passed two big lorries in a row without using my winkers.

'I think we've shaken them off,' I announced triumphantly.

I was ready to kick the bottom out of the car, only to get away from the spectre of this crazy pursuit, the burden I felt, of all the shadows weighing on our story, of all the deferred questions, from Marcel to that night with Sergino, and it could be anything, a car with a Marseilles registration, or private detectives set on our trail by someone who perhaps was still Joan's husband, or simply a hallucination we were both having, when, to give us the lie, the two yellow headlights showed in the mirror again.

'They've caught up on us, Joan.'

She looked at me, without a word, she was deathly pale.

'They have it in for you, don't they?' I questioned.

She shrugged, as she does, with a challenging air.

'I'd just like to see them follow us right to Venice.'

At the sight of the exit lane warning I let up on the accelerator, it was beginning to get dark and the car behind us was simply a grey blur. Now I knew it was them, the strangers who threatened Joan for some reason that would remain unknown to me. We ran along the causeway from Mestre, losing them and spotting them again, leaping forward to overtake and then lying hid, while a host of dark questions stood up on the horizon out of the mist over the lagoon.

You were listening hard, eye on the door, upon the handle, to that step which mounted the stairs and which you were learning to distinguish as hers or another woman's, all clandestine like us, at three in the afternoon, the minutes running, and you do not dare go up to the bed which is there to lay waste, you stand by the heater, with your coat still on, the shutters closed, Silver's voice from downstairs as she prepares the coffees, the voices of the few customers who come in, even the hiss and gurgle of the expresso machine, so deep is the silence of San Siro, an island of fallen leaves, of little villas, of boundary walls, and you think that she will not come, that she has grown tired, that it is just because of this that you have never desired her as today, and you reckon what everything else comes to, outside of this place, supposing Joan really does not come, another five minutes have gone, take a good look at these walls, at these pillows, because it is the last time, there, that was the phone ringing downstairs, it will be her saying she cannot, saying that he has not gone out, it has happened before, at the last minute, until at the sound of steps you have run out on to the landing, breaking every rule, because Joan is coming up breathlessly, we embrace on the stairs, but today she breaks free from the kiss at once.

'I can't stay darling, they have shadowed me, I made the taxi take a detour, but it didn't do any good, they are here downstairs . . .'

'Who?'

'I told you, he is capable of anything, even of calling in the police to catch us red-handed.'

'Are you sure?'

'Yes, I am. Their car is just outside over by the trees.'

'You've been rash, Joan, you shouldn't have come.'

'I don't care, I wanted to see you.'

The excitement of her skin, the perfume between her bare neck and her sweater, swaying like two blind people at the top of the stairs: over and above what we might have decided, our senses had already chosen, we crossed the threshold of the room, as if escaping from an ambush, aware that we had come to a turning-point and not worried by what it would presently cost Joan, whom a stranger was waiting for, in a car stopped over by the trees, this act of giving herself up with her own hands.

Silver led us out, an hour later, from the kitchen into a garden, they could fire at us, from the shadows of that back-shop, but, no, a lock was opened, and then a gate, and at once a chained Alsatian rushed at us barking, from behind wire-netting, we passed into the garden of an abandoned villa, unharmed, in the street there was only a stable-hand leading a hooded thoroughbred along by the halter, a deserted avenue flanked by poplars, and in the distance, but hostile, the city where we grew up.

* * *

No one should contemplate objects: their immutability, that undying character they have draws the blood from us, brings us close to death: under the rain I recognised the shining bronze of the Moors, beating out the hours with the same old motion, as I crossed over Piazza San Marco with Joan at my side, a desolate place today, thick with mistiness, much as I might have expected to find it, only, the bronze, its colour solid on the sky, was exactly the same, the impression, too, the same as the one I had kept of these very Moors and their gentle hammering, of the blows timed slowly in a square, as if ringing in memory, probably a honeymoon, an itinerary marked by snapshots at every bridge, but nine years have actually passed since that day and it is Joan you are now guiding down alleys and through little arcades, to the whistling, from nowhere, of a boy who will shortly come out in front of you: to the cries of the pigeons, to the quick beat of footsteps.

'I'm cold,' she said. 'Shall we drink a hot cordial?'

We looked behind us before entering, but no one seemed to be following: it was a restaurant with a bar that opened on to a square, we saw the back of a statue covered with pigeons, it was difficult to guess of whom, though there was the cocked hat and the frock-coat turned up in that way, I studied Joan's ankles against the walnut of the counter and my own wet shoes on the floor-boards, like actors on stage but not knowing their parts, thrown by our whim among the high voices of the boys who stood with their collars turned up, in the doorway, out of the drizzle.

'Why don't we stay here tonight too?' I suggested. 'I can write the article here, at the hotel.'

We turned round together as the bell over the door jingled, a short man came inside, wearing cloak and boots, he stared at Joan quite openly.

'Drink your cordial,' I said.

'It's scalding,' she answered, perturbed.

'What are you afraid of? You're with me.'

At last she seemed to give herself a shake: she finished her drink and we went out into the icy, fine rain, into the quarter opposite the one where we had arrived, towards Cannaregio, skirting other churches and stretches of blank wall, a Venice without gondolas, harsh and quick-moving, with few passers-by, Joan holding tight to my arm, well aware of the ambush lurking at every backwater, between one bridge and the next, in the silence of a boat-house, from a barge drawn up high, but going forward with fresh spirit, both on guard against the screeching of a lock or the rumble of a metal blind, the splash of a coble's oar as it steals along a canal, then hurried foot-falls on some steps or other, a basket with bread in it rolling out of an alley, we do not even know their faces and it could be any one of these people who are going their ways in a winter noon, an assassin who will follow us right to the Riva degli Schiavoni, then into San Marco, in the shadows of the basilica or on the steps before the bell-tower, he will see how I steal a kiss from her at every second step, from her lips that send up little clouds of warmth.

Again the city, with a whimsical turn, pushed us back to the lagoon, to the point we had set out from that morning, the Lido and San Giorgio veiled in mist, the water lapping the deserted landing stages, I held Joan's hand in the pocket of my overcoat as you grip a loaded revolver, a state of grace that makes up for every doubt, saturated with water ourselves but in well-being, like these little geraniums in tin-cans on the window-sills, the rubbish floating at the wide steps of the palaces, our blood is set flowing more swiftly because of the lagoon that is becoming sea, it throws up spray about the mooring piles and the ebb reveals how rotten their wood is, the hooter of a tug in the distance, then a long silence, not even the sound of our steps treading the large porphyry chips, I asked her: do you really love me, and there is a tolling of bells above us, a sodden tolling too, the privilege of standing there unspeaking to enjoy together every detail of that twilight of death without suffering any more from this decadence and the impossibility of an armed uprising, especially if, standing still in a portico, I can feel how Joan's womb throbs and the Grand Canal two feet away washes out and washes out again this huge wound.

'Not here, darling, let's go back to the hotel.'

We thrust the shutters wide, and the grey of the air, the rain, became the glow of dawn in an eighteenth-century room. Across from us, where the Lido just showed its misty outline, at the end of the string of lights hung over the lagoon, my father and my mother had just dared to touch fleetingly one Sunday in August.

I had to play it with cunning, not take anything head on, but turn up the cards of a game of patience at random, get her to admit, in some light mood, the reasons for her fears.

I had thought of it at Gleneagles in the Highlands, watching the last white-haired baronets playing golf as I sat in a easy chair upon the verandah of that Scottish castle transformed into hotel, a well-buttressed Victorian stronghold with its miles of corridor where shoes outside the door are burnished in the morning together with a copy of the *Financial Times*, a place that Joan would have taken to—the lights in the lifts and the orchestra in the dining room apart—I had thought about it in the dining-car as I came back to Edinburgh, after I had succeeded in collaring the film director at the eighteenth hole, and in making him repeat the banalities that I wanted for my readers' consumption, and finally at London Airport, waiting behind the plate-glass of the terrace for the transfer flight to Milan.

It was a message that I was already perfecting in mind, as alluring and treacherous as the signs that I had become the victim of, a sonata for harpsichord in which every phrase merged with the preceding ones as it liberated others, generating whole cascades of possibilities and towering up into a peak of fearful menace which I watched as it was endlessly made and unmade.

Consequently I had only to slip a sheet into my portable and type in capital letters:

YOUR LITTLE GAME HAS BEEN DISCOVERED IF YOU WANT DETAILS WRITE POSTE RESTANTE CAR LICENCE NO 73429/M.

I folded the sheet, put it into an envelope on which I had already written Joan's name and address with my left hand. I did not know if she would fall into the trap, but I was sure she did not know my licence number and that she was incapable of tracing it through the appropriate offices. At the letterbox I was tempted to give up the whole idea and tear the thing into little pieces, but posting it brought a sense of relief, something would happen, I would stop tormenting myself, I could attend to my work calmly, read a book again, without being distracted on every page.

The next day was Sunday. I phoned to arrange about seeing my daughter and took her to the zoo. She had had a chill with a temperature and was pale. She came to life a little as we watched the seals who enjoyed the cold and the fish we threw them, there was the feel of snow in the air, and we took refuge in a cake-shop. I tried to get her to laugh, but with little success: she watched me gravely, the cake half-nibbled, her little over-coat full of crumbs, as if she guessed that, as things were, I was going to be given an insight into Joan's true moods, her attitude to me, once she had my letter, and if my suspicions were without foundation, she would speak of them as a joke, something we could laugh at together.

But, no, three days passed without Joan's giving any sign of this. We went to the theatre one evening, and on our return she let me know I could stay the night. Her behaviour was so natural that I wondered whether she had got the letter. The next morning, on leaving her place, I called at the Central Post Office before going to the paper. I showed my licence to the clerk and waited for him to come back to the counter. I felt nervous, I kept looking round as if someone might surprise me in an act that I was the first to see as repugnant, I who had always made fun of symbols, words inscribed inside rings, laughed when I heard of medallions solemnly broken and the parts kept, of vows that tightened the finger on the trigger in the time of unfaithfulness, here was I waiting as if the answer of a Post Office clerk would be a sentence pronounced upon me and I studied the hands which still held my licence open.

'Nothing,' he said, handing it back to me, over the counter.

'Have a good look,' I had the nerve to say.

'Nothing,' he repeated.

I was almost happy, as if I had had proof of her innocence, of her patent, blameless indifference that no anonymous letter could shake. I gave up thinking about it for the whole day until, at eight in the evening, Joan called me at the paper to announce that she was going out of town.

'Where to?'

'Nowhere much, I'll be away two days.'

'Fine,' I said, 'have a good trip.'

She said nothing more. I felt her uneasiness. As for the words that I should have spoken and that I had in fact spoken in similar circumstances, I had no intention of pronouncing them now.

' 'Bye, darling,' she said at last.

I dined with Roberti and another fellow-reporter in the usual snack-bar, I went along with them to watch pelota, then to a café so as to be good and late. I had a job getting to sleep, and the next morning I called at the Central Post Office again.

There was an envelope, and as I lifted it, it seemed empty. In receiving it at the counter, my hands had trembled. As soon as I was back in my car, I tore it open. From it I drew out a sheet that bore a message made up of printed letters, cut out from a newspaper and pasted there.

It read: 'Dearest how can you think these things of me.'

The question mark and the name were missing: in her haste Joan had forgotten them.

By some tacit understanding we did not talk about this. It would have been for me, after all, to mention it, and I did not want to do that from a position of defeat, nor did I wish to discuss with her the reasons for my being so clumsy. Besides, there lay her little face, eyes closed in sleep, on the pillow six inches from my lips, and through the half-opened curtains of the french windows I saw the bare branches in the park, clean in the dawn of a clear, cold day, a show of strength, as reassuring as Joan's little jaw relaxed in slumber, the slight blowing from her nostrils, because we were late last night after I had got up and raced over to her place at one, it was the tone of voice when she telephoned, unexpectedly after less than twenty-four hours absence, not that she asked me to come over, on the contrary she merely said she was back and was I all right, nothing had happened to me, had it, I don't understand, I said, what it is that should happen to me, that's fine, she had said, who knows why I was anxious, and I felt a mad desire to take her hands in mine, squeeze them, twine fingers, as you do at times, in complicity, stroke her hand while I gave a long sigh of relief which I already felt growing inside me for the simple reason that Joan was here, come back, and she was even saying that she loved me, that she worried about me as if my life actually were threatened by someone or something which was not her, with her enigmas.

I was doubled up on my side, as I let myself slide closer beside her, Joan looked enormous, a solid figure unknown to solid geometry, on the branches the sparrows had begun their part-song, but I heard solemn classical music, there were pincers of chrome steel on a white napkin, the napkin was of sponge, marked with one or two dry blood stains, and the man who stood smoking near the window came up and said: *schnell, schnell*! to those who were busy strapping my fore-arms to the easy chair, and in a flash Joan took my place while the officer stood in front of her and stared at her through his monocle, his lips thin as a line as he inhaled in briefest puffs, he gestured for them to turn up the music, on the table there was an open jotter and a fountain pen beside the military hat, I did not see his face any longer because I was the officer and I walked up and down the room, my boots glistening on a floor of white and black tiles already seen somewhere, a strong smell of disinfectant, and the officer's voice came out of my mouth, as he swung round to face the chair.

'We have methods that would make the dumb talk . . .'

Joan smiled faintly in her sleep, the corners of her mouth drawn up so slightly at a fleeting vision of bliss, and this was intolerable, an insult to this uniform which anyone would pay for bitterly, and I myself hoped that she would bring herself to it, that it would not be necessary to begin, inside myself I was saying to her, speak, what's making you keep quiet, tell me where you have been, yesterday and on previous occasions, and who are the others, what is the pass-word, in any case we know everything already, it's useless for you to deny, come on now, speak, who did you see yesterday, speak, in any case Marcel has already confessed, you were in Paris and then? you have to tell us who you saw at Marseilles, the name, out with it, the name of the man who fired the shot on Avenue Garibaldi, and all right then, you don't want to talk, all the worse for you.

I gave a sign for them to begin, I had turned my back to her during the last part because I loathe the sight of blood when it begins to run from the finger-nail and the finger-nail is still attached to the flesh, but there was no time, because Joan threw herself into my arms, her breath touched my forehead entangling me in her sleep, she murmured something, an indistinct whisper, stay here, what's taking you to Paris, her hand reached for me, I knew I was lost.

From the wall the mask of the Basonge of the Congo which the witch-doctor wears in times of disaster, plague or war, fixed its eye on me with the shadow of a mocking smile where the sandalwood was cut right through. I had brought it back with some others from a voyage, years earlier, when I still enjoyed collecting mementoes, little figures in ebony, ceremonial masks, the crude symbols of what had been black Africa from the Transvaal to Chad, and what I could not get into my book.

'I've brought the papers for you,' Joan said.

'You're a dear, you think of everything, the whole time.'

'What did you tell them at the paper?'

'The truth: that I wasn't feeling well, so I could not make the trip.'

Now my fever had subsided, I began to feel like eating and like reading something too.

'You must have caught a cold in Paris the other day,' she added, as she slipped on her fur coat.

'You going already?'

'I'm expecting some Americans at the shop. If I can, I'll come up for a moment in the afternoon.'

She breathed a kiss on my forehead, she looked like a Florence Nightingale among the wounded. I said to her: you are Sister Joan of Sad-house.

'You see?' she answered. 'If we lived together, this is how it would end: a mutual aid society, like all marriages.'

And yet I still thought of it, I who had come out of conjugal existence a loser, thought of a way of living together with Joan, the chance of attempting it again, union with another, when my direct experience should have told me it was an illusion, or at best a makeshift. Perhaps because today I seemed to detect a yielding in her that was unexpected, which Joan granted me like a rare favour. I felt I was near the solution as her perfection and detachment melted in tenderness for me, and I held her hand against my cheek, not letting go, there, I said: if it were always like this, and I would have wasted away with consumption, day by day, to have her by me in this way to the end, I know who you are, I said to her, finally, rediscovering in her the

137

Joan of our clandestine time, the vehemence of our resistance, something never to be repeated.

I began to imagine things in the loneliness of my flat; the fog was still really thick and the cold made visible by that white frost on the panes, just as it was in that late autumn of 1928.

He has been living here for barely two months, in his rented room in Viale Piave, from the moment he came ashore on a platform of the Central Station with case in hand, into the traffic which must have made him feel even more alone, twenty-six thousand automobiles running in Lombardy, as against the ten cars or less that go about inside the circuit of those Swabian-built walls, the bad weather continuing throughout the whole of Upper Italy, goodbye sun of the Capitanata, the level of the River Po appreciably higher, the lake waters spilling into the streets of Como, even the Lambro in spate because of the torrential rains, it is probably because of this that he has a temperature and a chill just when he has found a job with an American firm and a first instalment of salary which will let him buy a silk-lined raglan at the month's end and black and white shoes which he has already seen in the window of a shop in Via Pattari, and gloves to hold in his hand, perhaps even a swagger cane, when the waitress of the bar downstairs next to the furriers' came up to bring him a white coffee and biscuits, I'm taking this up to that low-down Southerner who looks like Ramon Novarro, she told her boss, and she is a slender blonde, a gamine from Porta Vittoria here, and he eyed her the first time he ever entered the bar for a coffee and struck up a little conversation too, what was her name, but not at all, Ginetta's a lovely name, so she lays the tray across the wash basin and sits down on the only chair in the room, watches him sipping the hot white coffee, those emir's eyes above the wide rim are misted with his feverishness and she says take a biscuit or two, who knows what else she says, she laughs, showing every tooth in her head, she says all right, they will go to the Carcano Cinema together one Sunday to see the review, she'll tell her boy friend that she can't make it, she talks and laughs impulsively as the girls in this city do, not in the least shy because there is a man there standing in front of them, with the air of knowing all about it and in spite of that she will be the first girl from the Lombard-Venetian region to fall into his clutches, and no later than tomorrow, while crowds of loyal citizens swarm for the tenth Anniversary of the Victory, as work is ending for her, she will leave the bar on the pretext of taking him up a squash, and the record is turning and in the horn of the gramophone a voice is singing in husky tones while the hand knows where to bite gracefully, so that she can bring herself to give in, to get into the couch-bed with him, and share his fever, and bend her gamine's head back as my mother will do, on this same woollen blanket, six months from now, in the spring.

PART TWO

Wall Street had closed with a drop of almost sixteen points on the Dow Jones index, and this had made Joan a little nervous about some sterling she held, not that a fall in share prices can upset the moods of a woman in love, but her equanimity stemmed from economic security as well, a state to which she seemed biologically predestined.

So it struck me as just natural to accompany her on this expedition to the golf-practice range behind the Idroscalo, and then sit no distance away and look over newspapers while Joan on the driving ramp began dealing blows with her club, her feet set firm, altering her stance each time.

An agency message from Amsterdam spoke briefly of a forgers' establishment, discovered by chance in a basement of the public library there: a news item of no interest to anyone else and which I alone could link with Joan, with her behaviour that was irreproachable from the outside but which could mask any sort of underhand activity at all, in fact, it exhilarated me, this idea of her as the enemy of that society she belonged to without great strains or wrenching.

As for what I suffered myself in this way, I avoided talking of it just as you do not discuss an incurable disease. The old world that we had imagined we were fighting was taking us over day by day, and the new one provided better and better alibis for our powerlessness: therefore I was perfectly free to devote myself to Joan, to search in her at least for the oneness, the coherency found nowhere else. Through some mysterious action of time, the moment had come when our two fates seemed to join together naturally, completing one another, twin flasks by which only the best of ourselves would be decanted, a daily lesson that I was learning from Joan, from her unrivalled capacity for distilling moments of love as though they were drops of rarest essence. And certainly I admired her for the determination with which she translated into practice what for me were vague abstract principles.

She came up breathlessly to drink a cup of tea, I told her not to tire herself, knowing very well that she would not listen to me, and in fact she went straight back to take up her stance by the instructor and send golf balls into the grass with such zeal you would have thought this was her mission in life.

In this matter, I had to agree Joan was right: we had not to live together so as not to share the meaningless incidents of life in common, the domestic burdens, the yawning breaks that lead to habit and then satiety. And yet I was often nettled to observe that Joan was not troubled in the least by the loneliness that a relation like this ultimately condemned us to, never the hint of resentment in her voice when we said goodbye, so much so that I came to suspect—when in my turn I had to spend whole long evenings in the lounge of a hotel or alone at the theatre or dining with people I cared nothing for—that some purpose unknown to me kept Joan firm in her intention. In fact, as no material obstacle stood in the way of our coming together, I found I was brooding on this possibility more and more frequently.

Wilfully, I trusted to events: I had faith in what we build up in ourselves, what is fated to take place. And that was near now, very near.

The vertical motion of the drill, its point going up and down in the earth, stops one day, meets empty space, and that can be all. I had not one doubt, however: it was Marcel.

He was wearing a raincoat with the collar turned up and carried a small bag, he came towards me with that breezy confidence in his step itself, Marcel just come out of Joan's lift, he passed me in the entrance hall without a flicker of recognition, I went back to the door to watch him getting on to his motor-cycle van and then the van going off into the night, I was tempted to follow him, but at the same time relieved to think that something was at last ripening which Joan could not hide.

I paused before her door to draw breath and order my thoughts, or rather, my feelings, because I had to be very lucid, and Joan would throw me into confusion easily if she opened her arms, I would keep my eyes fixed on something solid and unmoving, and the truth was that what I kept seeing was the blotchy skin from that morning, the outlines of the scars on Marcel's back, with new and more conscious horror, I had not had the courage to stop him, to denounce him in his own language, to tear from his hand the little bag, like a doctor's, he, Marcel, come here out of hours, to visit Joan, to play the abject part with this woman, his employer, something I could well understand, a pretence that opened spy-holes upon lust and then chasms of perversion and madness.

'What's this, aren't you coming in?'

The voice, the appearance of Joan confirmed my fears about her, the easy wonder, the mask I had come to snatch away.

'What a surprise, I thought you had gone down to Rome . . . ?'

But, as things turned out, the paper had wired me to come back, I had no desire to start telling her all about it, anyway the news conference had been a piece of bluff that had taken in fellow-reporters too, but instead I was studying the ash-tray in which two cigarette ends of the brand Joan smoked had been stubbed out just before, and as I had never seen her smoke two cigarettes at once, I lifted the ash-tray and felt that the bottom of it was still warm.

'There's smoke here,' I said.

'You haven't even given me a kiss.'

She kissed me, and must have noticed that something was wrong.

'Would you like to go out? Are you staying here tonight?'

'There's smoke,' I said again. 'Have you had visitors?'

'No, why?'

This was what I expected, I walked away a step or two, to have room enough to stretch out my arm and take more careful aim. Then I said: 'What was Marcel doing here?'

'Oh,' Joan breathed again, tried to suppress a laugh, gave in and, laughing now, told me that the cap from her tooth powder had slipped down into the waste pipe of the wash basin, and since the water would not go away and as Marcel is a very good hand at plumbing and the actual plumbers themselves are never to be had, she had thought of calling him in and he had come with his tool-bag, it wasn't the first time, and there is nothing at all strange about it.

'Of course not: you go off, come back, disappear again, never explain anything, and there's nothing strange about it.'

There was pained surprise in her look that was like distress at her inability to be different, or simply at the melancholy spectacle of my smallness, and I had no more than begun.

'Try and understand: what meaning is there to my life? Running after you for ever and ever!'

Joan did not reply: she avoided giving me answers that we both had by heart, was unruffled as if she spoke from the other end of the wire, I could not even be sure that she saw me, a phone-call about business in which there is always one who runs and another who chases, only, I had never been used to the chaser's part.

'I'm tired, understand, I'm very tired. You know the life I lead, from train to hotel, to write things I often don't believe in, see people who don't interest me, only because I've a family to support.'

'You can skip that chapter, we know it.'

'All right. Now I want to put a little order into my life. Why shouldn't we live together, if it's true that you and I are different from the others? For ten days, let's try it.'

'Otherwise?'

She was standing near the french windows, she turned towards the panes, not to let me see she was

147

biting her lip.

'Otherwise we'll end by leaving one another.'

'You'll go back to your wife?'

'I didn't say that.'

'Fine, you didn't say it.'

We kept silent for a little while, I blew smoke down at the carpet, Joan turned her back on me, a gesture reminiscent of a middle-class comedy.

'Man, any man, needs a lair.'

You could even hear the dull roar of the cars outside. Joan turned round: her eyes were wet with tears.

'Do you think it would help you, that you would work better if you were to live with me? Would you complete your unfinished masterpiece?'

I shrugged. To me the book on Africa mattered little, considering the point we were at.

'I only think that we should take the risk, that it is right to try. I don't care what you do, but I have the right to protect you.'

She walked towards me, I was ready to take her in my arms, ask her pardon for this moment of thoughtlessness, to swallow every word I had said. But no, Joan changed direction, went and lit a cigarette, began walking about with short, troubled steps, came back in front of me, her eyes quite dry, sure of herself again.

'All right: we'll try. You bring your things here. But straightaway, before I think better of it.'

I took ten days from the holiday still owing to me from the previous year, and I settled in at Joan's. It

148

was like getting back to the summer before at Portovenere, in her house, with my clothes hanging by hers.

She had been surprised by this decision, but she had accepted it with a good grace for the sake of the book that I could finish in those ten days. Her flat was not big, but furnished with exquisite simplicity, I was at my ease there, I had a work table set for me before the french windows of the living room, and round about, objects, ornaments that were already familiar to me, and in my typewriter, on that first morning, a white sheet awaited the first taps of a new story, say history.

I had decided to rewrite the first part completely, concentrating this time on political manoeuvres executed behind the scenes, using the documentary material that I had gathered for the purpose in the course of my travels, testimonies and enquiries, cases of blackmail and conspiracies that I had not been free to write about in my paper.

It was raining, Joan took leave of me hurriedly, I wanted to keep her back, but it was after nine, the door closed behind her, I stayed there listening to the hiss of the lift as it went down. I looked at the rain-water with gratitude, the white sheets of paper, now I was waiting for Joan with the passion of our first days, when it was secret, I compared what I felt then with what stirred me now and then both states with the rain, the collective drama, the November flooding, my first coverage after our private love story began, and I had had to go off in a hurry, without being able to warn her as I was afraid a simple phone-call might make her husband suspicious, but then the phones themselves were not working, Florence flooded and the coastal plains too, a tragedy I still kept a few notes on.

Immobile on the two banks of the canal they watched the eddying in silence, men in rubber boots, women with children in their arms, under big green umbrellas, staring at the spate, a calf still on its feet, in the middle of the flow, in the groaning of the boats, gunwale to gunwale, then every so often a sharp thump, like a shot, and it is another bit of earth falling away, a house wall collapsing, and watch Silvano's boat, it's turned right over already, all Marina is there along the course of the Fossino which has carried away the bridge at its mouth, and in front of the cathedral the water is almost six feet deep, the boys excited as if it were all fun, the buzzing of the helicopters, no passage this way, says the inspector, on the Aurelian highway the pallid girls under the rain, come out of their houses to watch their chickens and turkeys floating in the pre-dawn light, now they take another end of the line and tie the boat up at a cement pier, try by the roadfork, the inspector says, and as the Ombrone has already broken its banks at two points, there is an express bus filled high with water and the passengers all on the roof waiting for the police helicopter, the telegraph poles which are afloat, their wires crossed, skeletons in that sea of mire, and it deluges down without end, even the sea is hectic red with the washed-down clay, the streets as if there had been a battle, and it is not finished yet, lucky that the wind has shifted to the north and the sea is receding, the sea that has already carried off all the boats, the howls of the women on the steps of the farm buildings, made islands in the vastness of this lake that is still growing, the iron bars, the uprooted trees, rubble of death in the dark that is coming down, and the sun of the new day in mockery of the disaster, the turkey-cocks perched on window-sills, on cart wheels, on the corpses gathered by the boats: that we loved another, that Joan loved me had seemed a crime.

Today when we were paying for our double liberty in other ways, today I could acquit myself. An occasional glance at the world was enough to convince me, and anyway it was little changed since little men with boyish faces who we like to think are different from us, with other bones and affections, barefoot or in plastic sandals had lain low in the rice fields, weighed down with TNT, waiting for the tanks; as they breathed through a cane, living for months like sewer rats, and we were in a rented room, wearing ourselves out in the sweetest unarmed combat, with an increasing awareness that none of these secret meetings would ever contribute to the collapse of the West, and if anything this is your fear: that nothing will change, that events will deride your faith in history. And the beetles that came out of my father's shoes in the room in Viale Piave are the same ones that you were to find, as you came home in the evening, in another boarding house, as soon as you pressed down the light switch, the black cockroaches that defy wars and revolutions, as resistant to death as the plague-spreaders—the 'smearers'—on the wheel.

Of the two of us Joan had come out of the encounter almost unscathed. I had this, too, to learn from her: how to make myself a warrior, put on armour, go back on to the glacis of the castle, the supplier of munitions or caster of mortars, take up my position again during the days of siege, beside her in the creaking of the winches, Joan of Arc in a coat of mail, her loose hair spreading as she rode, the same gaze as she has today, and it is a photo of her as a girl at the riding-school of San Siro, that has come from a drawer.

I shut the drawer again, feeling guilty. I went back to my papers, the sheet slipped into the typewriter was still white. I knew I did not have long: in a little while the cleaning woman would ring. I opened the drawer once more, there was a whole box of photographs that Joan had never shown to me, perhaps realising that for me the series of enigmas moved from here, the answers to questions not to be escaped, the key to her mysterious present.

She was on horseback, bare-headed, her lips drawn in a contrite expression as she faced the camera, and the hint of a smile in her gaze, there were other figures in the background leaning on a fence, but blurred, perhaps relatives of hers, perhaps a youth among them who would steal a kiss from her as soon as she dismounted, and the distance between us had never shown so great as in this photograph in which I vainly tried to place myself, I let her go round the track at a little trot, I followed that innocent heaving of hers, the boots gripped to the side of the beast, I waited for her to pass in front of me again but I did not manage to catch her eye because Joan seemed to be unaware of us, looking straight in front of her at the horse's ears, but not proud, only distant, inaccessible like the

Countess Alice behind the bars of the gate, in her villa in Valbrone, and now you know only too well what your part has always been: bastard of a Spanish prince, stable lad, stirrup holder, chamberlain waiting for the chance to lay hold of this daughter of the lords of Milan, she will know you by your step, by your stride as one of her people, quite worthy of her as she throbs in her dress after the gallop, a nunnish white in that lace colour, her, warm against the hilt of your basket-handled sword, so white, the neck of Sister Virginia de Leyva and how it bends to your lips the moment she is taken and crushed in the window niche, in the wild folds of a hanging, and her girl's skin already has that smell you know, there is a long corridor with hexagonal tiles that shine, where the beat of heels echoes, silver clasps like the hilt of a dress-sword, here is violence come back, like a blood calling, the broad hat with its plume, halberds and falchions and lances and pikes which hem her in, the gurgling of a fountain, light and shade on carved marble, here are the implements, the lantern and the dice, her uvula throbs in the gorget of organza, the huge oak screw turns in the board and the rope tightens, a strappado for the one who dared to approach this daughter of noblemen, but who she is, you will really never know, now you can shout to the torturer that you have never known, as Joan entered Sad-house to become a novice, penitent and calm in the lurching saloon that was taking her there, like someone going to expiate a sin of love.

You see her going, behind the crude fencing, then a bell rings—the woman come to do the cleaning—

twice, three times, it shook you back, until the next enchantment.

It had stopped raining, minute stalactites dripped from the balustrade of the balcony outside, we were in the living room, smoking over our coffee cups, and I had to admit that I had not progressed by a single page, that morning, thanks to the different landscape that encircled me, I could not confess to her that I had opened a drawer that was not mine, in which there lay a box full of photographs she had never shown me, divining the reason for this only today, that is, her fear that I might catch some fragment of truth from those adolescent images, create the part of her that I still needed, and which Joan insisted on hiding from me as something exclusive and, I was free to suppose, shameful too.

At this point something occurred to me that I had not considered before: Joan could certainly have kept a maid, and yet she preferred a daily woman who was quite old, someone from outside with neither eyes nor ears, who would never wonder about Joan's behaviour, in the house or away from it. Moreover this discovery, suddenly taking on a significance, fitted into the picture of the other clues, it illuminated the dark places there, like an additional proof of guilt, bearing out the original charge against her. I was forgetting that it was Joan, if anyone, who was to reach a verdict by the end of those ten days.

We fell asleep together, straight after lunch, as naturally as any young couple. Lying down fully clothed, Joan at once kindled my desire for her. She yielded beautifully, then I held her hand while we drifted sleepwards again, I made out new suggestions in the shadows which the top of the light shade projected on the ceiling, until I was lost in a maze of guesses and glass drops from Murano, Joan's bosom falling into a quieter rhythm now, I was interpreting the first skirmishes of what, from this time on, could grow into habit, glad that no sign of it showed, that she kept, just like a wave curled upon itself, the mystery in herself inviolable.

At four in the afternoon she woke up, horrified, made what haste she could to go out, urging me to work at my book, but there was a slowness in her motions, the beginnings of laziness, an after-effect of love-making, I had never noticed in her before. I promised: the afternoon was turning fair, patches of clear sky between the tree's dry fingers, the coasts of Africa almost visible, blue and hazy as if with the heat shimmer, I put things together laboriously, I crossed out a sentence, and I had almost got going when the phone rang, a long, unusual ring, and then a voice saying, hello, into the receiver, and it was Amsterdam that wanted Joan, the operator again and at last a man asking for her in bad French.

'Madam is not here, but I can take a message.'

I seemed to have alarmed him, there followed a crackling in the earpiece, I said hello a few times, I was cut off, my hands were sweating, the feeling of being near to a revelation, near to what I would have to do so that the truth could be known.

I glanced at my watch. Joan would just have reached the shop, I was tempted to call her and tell her what had happened, it was obviously the right thing to do, but I did not want to spoil the chance of learning something about her, and not as a matter of curiosity now but much more, mine was a fever to know, a questioning that devoured me. I could speak about it at dinner in an offhand way and watch her reactions, wait until she exposed herself, but by this time some notorious quarters of Amsterdam were coming back to me, the *graht* behind the old town centre where I had once seen the provos fight it out with the police, the smell of those lanes, the girls displaying themselves in those interiors like goods in shop windows, the drug pedlars, all these contributed suggestions for a character who was far from imaginary, and the less this character resembled Joan, the more likely the identification looked to me, it was a play of mirrors which, reflecting the same image, insensibly distort it, and you walk about the room, touch an ash-tray, switch on and off a lamp, and the room becomes narrower and narrower, it presses at your back, a stage-set complete with wings and backcloth for a part you chose to play that is now grotesque, now in the twilight key, and which all the time you had thought of as vibrant, a headstrong role of a revolutionary quickly stifled by the passing days, where on earth is the freedom fighters' sierra and where, the barracks overrun by the citizens, at the moment you stand before a little Louis Quinze mirror and what you see is the portrait of a Milanese gentleman, and no question about it, you would have worn a grand wig, a three-cornered hat, fine stockings and buckles to your shoes, discussing liberty and justice at the café and in the end have a little book published under an assumed name and circulate it in the salons of this little court that embraces us, I and Joan who has come out once more from the bottom of the box, a photograph folded in two, as if it had been saved from destruction at the last minute, now I rummaged among her things without restraint, I was looking for a proof of her guilt though I knew I would not find it, and she is laughing behind her mask, dressed as an eighteenth-century lady among faces I do not know at a Milanese carnival party, her silvered hair combed high and shining, she laughs behind her fan, I tried to date the image, perhaps five years earlier, and it must have been this one that her husband had been about to tear to pieces, the next moment, instead, he had caught and slapped Joan, being blind with jealousy, with her laughing behind her fan, and he does not understand that she is mocking me too, mocking all my imaginings about her, as though that were the highest manner of loving.

It was five, the musical clock in the hall gave out its little theme, regular with the hour, filling the rooms with an indefinable sound, the waves going out over the little persian carpet, reverberated by the walls, absorbed by the velvet of the arm-chairs, and it is so natural for Joan to choose a costume like this as fancy dress, almost presaging my arrival: one day I would look at her from a distance, as I mixed with the crowd, an unknown subject of the Imperial court, see her, in that dress, get down from a carriage and go into La Scala with the same indifference with which, had she been born elsewhere, she would have mounted the few steps to the platform and raised her eyes up to the blade.

I felt she was getting away from me, as if she had scattered her track with false clues, the track I had been following for months now, but there were drawers and other receptacles to visit, because in the nine days left me before Joan gave her verdict, I was going to learn her secret. Never had I loved her so much as in this act of profanation.

'I don't know, I can't even guess. In Amsterdam I met quite a few people. All different. Probably he's one of the antique dealers.'

You wonder how she can do it: her coolness, not one bat of an eyelid, never a start.

'No, wait, I've brought some ice-cream.'

And how you might catch her out, find a chink in her perfect armour.

'Why don't you tell the truth, Joan?'

Flattered, she rises up to hug me, she wants to know if the afternoon has been so very long without her, she sits on my knee relaxing completely, and so erases the words I had rehearsed for her, I wanted to pretend that the voice had added a brief message, something like '*nous attendons Van Gogh*', I think it was, which would certainly have done and would perhaps have disconcerted Joan, but which, in the end, struck me as ridiculous as my doubts did, in the downpour of her hair, flowers in the tall vase on the table still laid, we could go to a film, or to bed with a glass of whisky, our books, a good record, the happiness from little things—because we will not attain the great—the very things I had renounced.

'Let's go to bed, of course.'

I was signing a truce, I was well aware of this, every time I savoured the freshness of the sheets with her. A truce not only with myself, to hell with all suspicion, but with the aggressive relationship Joan forced on me, with that ceaseless striving, that furious pursuit of her.

'How do you feel?' she smiled, as she settled her pillow.

'Would you rather have gone to a film?'

'Of course not,' she said. 'I like watching you read . . .'

She broke off, as if regretting a phrase that was not her, or rather which she thought out of place, we had spent the night hours through till dawn discussing this, getting at the true significance of habit and innate preference, and the causes for the reverse that, for different reasons, we had both suffered in the matter of living in common, until we had come to regard that as something we could not allow.

'I have been thinking of all the times I've slept with you, and tonight seems the first.'

'You're not going to feel too much of a husband?'

'A husband would want to know who rang you from Amsterdam. And everything else.'

Joan did not answer, opened her book, but I knew that she was only keeping her eyes on it, without reading. It was her way of telling me that I was making a mistake, but perhaps the biggest error was something else: it was wanting to share everything with her, to see her rise and dress, undress and lie down, only so I could be convinced that she was of human proportions, and I was seized with the suspicion that even that would not be enough, that Joan would stay inaccessible, the headland of Portofino faded in the mist of nightfall, there was perfect silence, the air unmoving, the eye of the lighthouse darting on the water every three seconds, and that still air you get just before a disaster: what will become of us, I thought, and then the night that we spent in that motel with trains passing directly under it, first a distant roar, then the boom which shook the night to vanish as quick into the mountain's side, and the few other times we had come together, after days of conspiring, all along the different routes of my journeys, secret meetings on which the secrecy itself and the shortness of the time conferred anxiety and splendour, an afternoon when a storm was coming, the sky pressing on our bodies, when the universe has shrunk to one hollow, bundles of black cloud weighing down, babbling the last words of our story because that is what they seemed to us at every rendezvous, frenzied and bewildered under the first drops that rattled on the windows, saying over my love, my love, with the stabbing light of the first thunderflash behind the slits in the shutter, and going out from there it was our lifeless bodies we dragged, the truer part of us stayed, desperately inside those walls, in silence right to the first station, did you notice, we broke the ash-tray, Joan had said as we went out, like a sinister omen, the pieces of chinaware on the floor of a room we would not see again, I held the umbrella over us with one hand and my case in the other, already tied to Joan by tender knots, laced cords of love, knots of love doubled through the sail's whipped eye, so we could resist every snatch of wind together, and even

Joan herself, her outward firmness, the precision of her gestures, came out of this a little sea-worn, as if she had risen up from that bed tainted, weakened, disarmed, in the little passage to the station.

'My man,' she said. 'Gravely reading.'

I felt her at my side, I stretched an arm to encircle her, the paper with my latest article in it had ended up on the bedside rug, she said that I had to stop writing about things that did not interest me, and finish my book soon, and then a great many other books, her hand stroking me deferentially, until we found ourselves with the lights all out, in the silence of an ambush thick with sighs, we were lying down head to foot, and as a landscape that you travel back over the opposite way reveals an outline so different as to appear quite new, so Joan's body looked quite unknown to me or at any rate full of unknown features in the light of our stubs, in the red glare like signal rockets above a mountain, verey lights in the darkness: the more so because action at night makes it easier for you to move up close to the positions to be attacked and also gives you a better chance to move about in territories little known to you, and so my hand having come back victorious from its reconnaissance, I could make out the thick of the underwood, I estimated the forces and the fire power: far off, the hills of that bosom quiet in the dark, beyond no man's land.

When I awoke, Joan had already gone. I went to the bathroom and pulled out the plug: it was broad daylight, the stripped branches of the chestnut-trees white with rime, and I wondered how I had managed to sleep so deeply as not to hear her rise and move about the room, a sign that Joan had taken every care. Realising this, I felt flattered for a little, then more and more annoyed as the minutes passed. It was as if I had been tricked while I slept.

On the flat of the wash-stand a landslide of little flasks, bottles of cologne left deliberately open and their tops scattered among the cosmetics and per-fumes were the only earthly trace of her passage. From a hook hung the night dress, embroidered and trimmed with lace, that I had given her before I knew that Joan hated sleeping with anything on. I took it down, I could practically bunch it in my fist, I caught the perfume of her skin from it.

Once again the real happenings of our past life together seemed shadowy before those which imagina-tion evolved as the only true ones.

I was looking for shoe polish and brushes in a cup-board in the bathroom when out of it rolled a hand-book of sorts, an old, rumpled manual in English. The title said: The Working of Diamonds.

I had never been so near the truth and at the same time so tempted to run away from it, siding with that instinct that makes us fly from a painful cer-tainty. I had the manual on my work-table beside my typewriter into which I had slipped the first sheet of the day, and I hesitated to study the thing for fear of coming across the verdict there that I would then be fated to pronounce on Joan, because now the reason why she was reluctant to live together was clear, reluctant at least until she was sure of me, knew I would not dare ask questions, violate her private life, demand an account of her absences for no apparent purpose. Now that I could sew the thin work of my guesses together, real elements in the matter suggested other terrifying deductions, that were certainly borne out by experience, because the chief centres for the cutting of precious stones are just Amsterdam and Anvers, and the shop in Milan, the dealing in antiques which, after all, could yield Joan little or nothing served as a cover for the other trafficking, what are you doing? I was saying to her: she was bent forward as she examined the quality of some precious stones with an eyeglass, and you, on tiptoe, were spying on her from the doorway, she kept a little pair of scales beside her, and wore the night dress you had given her, a small light burning there, and she did not seem aware of my presence, perhaps, you thought, she has found the Koh-i-noor, but her shoulders hid the thing she was studying, I heard a door bang shut and then a motor starting up, I need only have looked out and I would have seen Marcel on his motor-cycle van, I knew a place in Montmartre, Rue Germain Pilon, where they did electric tattooing 'without pain', across from a little hotel that was a brothel, it was there that Marcel had skulls and daggers, talons and women's lips, traced on his biceps, and at the moment he is holding something under his arm, perhaps a violin case, perhaps Franchetti's self-ejector shut in its gun-case, I should have understood right from that morning at the shooting ground, he is the one who supplies the weapons, all the pieces fit now, even Silver falls into place, with her convenient rooms behind the race-course, and you had been nothing but a pretext, probably there has not been one bit of reality in what we have lived, it was Joan's husband calling her from Amsterdam, his, the mysterious presence overshadowing us, and their separation could hide something quite different from what was thought, a labyrinth where I still beat about, determined to protect in Joan the supreme chance of a love, not only those shoulders, beautifully rounded, which are bent over something unknown which may not even be diamonds: take away the stone and you uncovered an abyss.

And yet, after no more than three days of life in common, Joan's face began to take on another look, the firm, decisive features betrayed a sort of easing, a softness I had never seen in her, and some way this justified my presence in her house. Meanwhile, my loneliness was turning me into a seer, I had the power to discern, in the long afternoons which I spent in fantasies, the hidden side of things. At last I succeeded in detaching myself from the shadow of the past to give myself over entirely to questioning the present, so much more alive and baffling, and the present was still her, Joan. Even when I looked through the morning papers distractedly, every item seemed to involve her, linked us with an epidemic in Nepal, a new outbreak of flooding in Setchuan, or one more earthquake in the Philippines, a whole train crashed down a mountainside in the Cordigliera, and the number of peon dead runs to hundreds, curt headlines occupying three columns folded beside the bottle of mineral water, the way I had seen this done in restaurants for years now, and this time they concerned us too, through her I was recovering the lost revolution, because the miracle Joan worked was to increase my receptivity, she multiplied the ways in which you could understand the world and those of its manifestations that I had detested and from which my strength grew, the uncompromising stance I had lost, the names of the commemorative streets that we would have changed: a square for Saint-Just, an avenue for Trotsky, and, under the name, the inscription 'revolutionary', in place of the philanthropists and false patriots who, I could see from Joan's aristocratic windows, were immortalised at the council's expense.

So you stood within the fortress, you gazed at the landscape from the height of those walls that you had considered unscalable in those days when Joan used to play exercises on the piano each afternoon, but already getting ready to be different, weighing the hypocrisy of these gestures and the good reasons for which she would choose a husband from among the men of her own world, but not knowing that to stay at his side would mean being mutilated, being killed by habit, as had happened to me too.

I tore myself from the window, the phone was a step away: I rang Joan, hoping with all my strength that she had not gone out. The girl who was her assistant answered, would I wait because Madam was attending a foreign customer.

'I'm sorry, but it's urgent.'

After a few seconds I recognised her step as she came quickly towards the phone.

'Who's speaking?'

'A friend,' I said, disguising my voice. 'Madame Joan?'

'Speaking.'

'Good: please be at Silver's at five.'

I hung up, waited for Joan to call me back, and in fact the phone trilled immediately.

'What's got into you?'

'Nothing: I want to see you.'

'At Silver's?'

'Yes,' I said. 'At Silver's.'

'Darling, you're not joking, are you?'

There was a tremor of joy in her voice, and I was still savouring this as I drove through the park heading for San Siro. It began to grow dark, I switched on my headlamps. We had never had a rendezvous at this hour in winter, and I had difficulty in recognising the open area and Silver's place, only two stories high.

Joan had not arrived yet. I went in, the café part was deserted, I had to knock on the kitchen door, and, after a long pause, Madame Silvia at last appeared, she recognised me and smiled, half in sadness, as though I reminded her of better times, and in fact she told me how her husband, who was the licensee, had been in jail a year already for contravening the ban on the letting of rooms to minors, but there was always a place for us, and I decided I would go up and await Joan there.

Half-way up the stairs I ran into a couple who were coming down, they had a sombre look, which I recognised as the selfsame one as we had had in those days the solemnity in the half-distracted gaze, of people who are condemned or who are getting ready to go back to prison after a brief spell of liberty, I turned the door handle and possessed our room again with its close and vaguely perfumed air: the basin on the tripod stand that Joan liked, hid by a screen, and the white porcelain jug, poor utensils to heighten her fragrance, and I am the surgeon who is at Ca' Granda, waiting for the cardinal's visit, because the Lazaret is already overcrowded with the plague-stricken and now there are some of them right in the entrance porch of this hospital, and in the court-yard where the medicine warehouse is, there are tubs full of bloody rags while the great bronzes toll for the feast day of the Pardon.

Then Joan advanced from the end of the corridor in the white habit of her order, the proud oval of her face, its pallor bound by the wimple, once again acting up to the part which has been forced on us, to be played out among these wretches who raise themselves up in their cots to kiss the crucifix she carries in her belt, and perhaps not even we are free of it, if fever of another kind devours us, a fury like an ague, a disease which mounts from the guts to search out our hands, while I held the scalpel, the speculum of silver, or the scrapers, there was a brief rattle and then silence, I lanced their swellings, twining her fingers, Joan's, with mine under a sheet all dirtied with blood, down from the arched windows poured a glaring light, and faces, almost purple in it, beg for hot oil mixed with yolk of egg to mitigate the pain from the lumps, and poppy oil, opium, mandrake, and they too have guessed how white that skin, her wantonness betrayed by her step, it is in this, then, that we recognised one another, she of noble blood, who had already given herself before she took her vows, a corrupt novice who sets your blood on fire with that Spanish glance, and already you despair of ever having her, surgeon barber, notorious among the scholars of Madrid who know nothing about gangrene, or of the blood letting which is more efficacious if the moon cannot be seen above the horizon, nor of how much pus you can get from their sores, since it would be fairer to let them die, and we heard their laments, the stench of the plague, the laughing of the helpers as they hugged us, their shirts spattered with ointments and poultices that went putrid on the wounds, the laughing of the helpers in the Giazzera courtyard, and at last we bare ourselves before the flasks, the alembics, the jars of bismuth, zinc and antimony in the ducal pharmacy, the entrance watched over by men-at-arms in breast-plates, Joan who are you, you panted running your hand over her, and she was wearing a little pouch of mysterious powder at her neck to ward off contagion, don't ask me any questions, she answered, and the next day you brought her a lodestone that had been blessed so it would cast out the devil that had possessed us both, and every day carts bringing new loads of the plague-stricken, and now the cardinal appears, we all fall on our knees, and every wailing dies, we must pray, Joan repeated, she avoided meeting me until one day on the stairs that lead to the wards I ran into her, as she was bringing towels, and once more she was mine, with the horror, this time, of the dissecting table on which she leant, her head hidden in the crook of her arm, and on the board the implements, the saws, my culter falcatus penetrating the sweetness of her, who-

168

ever you are we'll have to run away, I murmured, and the last night I dared to stay, naked, we were protected from every gaze by her unstained screen, inside the great sheet wrapping the camp bed, and that basin, the tripod, the towel and the arms of her family, the divine eye at the crossing of the vault unleashed, there we were, our thirst for life.

'Here I am,' she announced from the doorway.

She shut the door again, leant her back on it as she always did. In her arms she cradled a bottle of champagne bought on the way, she said: we must celebrate, but she was short of breath, she gazed at me and held the bottle against the breast of her raincoat.

'Have you noticed?' I said. 'Nothing has changed.'

I went up to take the bottle from her hand, Joan caught me to her almost with violence, she said, darling, she said: quick, take me quick.

You will ring the door bell. Just as a river that has been in spate comes back to its bed again, you will find shores again, voices, the family sounds, how long the seconds between that distant ringing and the thrusting wide of the door, and, inside, all the time that has run. From the table, laid for two, your daughter will lift her head and stare at you, without understanding. At this wonder the bells will ring, haloes will light as if by magic, tears of happiness under the Christmas tree.

How many times you called back that image, every single thing in its place just as you left it, years earlier. But then there was a break, other quick camera-shots in which the child is asleep and we, silent again, nothing heard except the sudden faint rustle of a newspaper as a page is turned, the sound of a piano just penetrating through the wall, the needle on the depth gauge rising, a hundred, a hundred and ten, a hundred and thirty, and the water closes back over us again, not even the walls will echo when you strike them now, everything is blunted, wadded in great silence and the only sign of life is the child's breathing.

'I see,' I said. 'I'll phone in the next few days.'

She had a temperature and a cough, there was no point in my forcing her to come out so I could see her, the more so when I let whole weeks go by without putting in an appearance, I wouldn't die if I even had to wait a few days, and who knows how this child is going to grow, moreover they had not received the monthly cheque yet: we haven't a thing, and that's the truth, so that I would feel the burden more keenly, the responsibility of that plural, but I did not want to depress myself discussing problems that made me feel low, because I had decided, on this third day of cohabitation with Joan, to devote myself to the book quite calmly.

In the rooms there was a pungent scent of mimosa which Joan had put into vases all over the place, an aquarium opacity lightened by the sun, itself invisible in haze, I was in the heart of the fortress, but not for long: in exactly one week Joan would pronounce sentence. This thought was disquieting. I laboured to fill two sheets. A sudden need for action drove me to lift the phone: I called the paper, there was nothing new, but I left Joan's number just in case. Probably

I'd never finish this damned book, and anyway there was no need for it, as far as posterity was concerned. It happens: that a knot of feelings and commonplaces prove stronger than reason, take on the force of solemn warning. I broke off to think about my daughter, something that had not happened for a good while, until I was assailed by the most ignoble of sentiments, great pity for myself, I had run through my paper and was looking for more in a little cupboard: I came across a pack of postcards held together by an elastic band, it was strange that Joan should keep any, I recognised the main square of Zagreb, the old trams and the skyscraper, then I turned the whole pile over and discovered my signature on the correspondence side of the bottom postcard: they had all been sent by me, and this one from Zagreb was the first I had sent with my name on it, after Joan had left her husband and set up house on her own, so the melting mood which thought of my daughter had induced in me changed into memories of love, I got back the unmistakable smell of coal dust in the wind sweeping the town, the old Vienna-type cafés, the scarves, the woollen gloves, I looked through the whole series of postcards, one after the other, and each one brought back a moment of our story, this romantic, unpredictable turn in Joan filled me with tenderness; there was a view of Aberdeen with the usual herring boats, the hundred ways of cooking a duck, and I could not even remember what job this one had to do with, but her last words at the airport, yes: I'm worried lest you tire yourself, she had a temperature that showed in the droop of her mouth, I travelled the exultant stages, departures, returns, right up to the most recent of them: a postcard from Dakar, another from Gibraltar, the one I sent as a joke at Portovenere the summer before, even the telegram from Lausanne station.

My letters were missing, probably Joan kept them somewhere else, and anyway I would not have re-read them, seeing my plans had changed so much from what they were. It was only now that the progress of our relationship took on definite shape, cold clinical charts from which the mystery of some of the circumstances, the shortcomings in her behaviour, bulked more largely, so much so that I had been led—I who had never believed it possible—to settle in beside her, to renew a contract of feelings most willingly, and it was also one of ways and habits. My profession had taught me how to make the effort to understand what is behind appearances, but everything regarding Joan was an uncrossable boundary, I battered at it desperately, every episode coalesced with another in a succession, the meaning of which I could not read, and perhaps it had none, Joan was simply mad, or I was, or both of us, and I had only a few days left in which to resolve this, now that I had managed to penetrate her private territory bodily, I was right in the middle of the enemy's camp, ready to strike, like a Greek in the belly of the horse, but I do not know where, at what point, if anything it should have been enough for me to discover that Joan, against all previsions, was resurrecting a desire in me to fight it out, had woken a frenzied wish to prove myself which till then I had known only at the beginning of a new love, when Aldina still resisted me, on the stairs up to her house, a desire that made me forget every anxiety, and it was the old man coming to the surface again, the warring man, the stud male, from that miserable couch in that room in Viale Piave upon which he, my father, had gambled away his life.

'Did you see the child?'

When she comes in and puts her arms around me, it is as if she came from a long way off; on her skin, in her voice and in her eyes she brings strange traces, the echo of something she has seen and breathed in who knows where.

'No,' I said, 'she had a chill.'

I tried to hide what was left of my irritation, but Joan had already read it in my look.

'Perhaps we should go out for dinner: you've been cooped up here all day.'

She changed, chose a dress I specially liked, I was about to tell her about discovering the picture postcards that afternoon, quite by chance, and how glad I was that she had kept them, but I decided it might arouse her suspicions.

'Any phone-calls?'

'None, Madam. Amsterdam has not rung so it's clear today that . . .'

She turned her head towards me, the eyes half made-up. Joan of Arc had vanished: in her place was Joan the Mad, the wretched Queen of Spain.

'So it's clear today that . . . ?' she repeated.

I was on the point of saying: they have arrested them, the diamond smugglers, spies, the forgers for whom she worked, the gang that had been printing bank-notes in the cellars of the Amsterdam public library, every one of them covered, as she was, by a fictitious profession, by a sacrosanct aura of respectability, income, propriety and good manners.

'Nothing,' I said, 'I was joking.'

She smiled with obvious relief, went on to say that Franchetti had invited us over to his place, after dinner, to play bridge.

'Do we have to?'

'Well, we never see anyone.'

'I like it this way. I have you. The others don't interest me, I'm already seeing too many people in the course of my work.'

'Just as you say, darling,' Joan said, closing the subject.

I was grateful to her for the way she could dispel the least hint of the matrimonial tiff: squeezing her waist as she gave me her short, fierce hug, I had the clear certainty that I would never tire of her.

'Help me to pull up this zip.'

She turned, offering her half-naked back to my eyes, I took the minute catch between two fingers, I had already begun to pull it upwards when, between the still-open edges of the dress, I saw it.

'What's the matter?' she asked.

It was a purplish mark on her skin between her shoulder and the base of her neck.

'One day I'll do an exposé of you, Joan.'

'For God's sake!' she laughed. 'Will you zip me to the top?'

'And so we'll know at long last how you get yourself these bites on the shoulder . . .'

I just could not joke about it: I had to struggle

with myself so as not to shake her, question her, slap her, use force, to make her confess the truth to me, from the beginning to the end.

Now Joan had turned her back to the mirror, was looking over one shoulder at herself, without a tinge of red, as if checking to see if her stocking seams were straight, and certainly leaving my indignation to dangle over the void.

'Answer me, damn it!'

'Can't you see for yourself? I've a lover.'

'I'm not joking, Joan.'

'Well, then, give it a rest!'

She knew how I hated appearing jealous and she was counting on that, ready to say 'just like my husband' at the first sign of rage, because no circumstances are so extraordinary that a gentleman has to get ruffled: consequently we went out, took her car, Joan sat at the wheel, merely asked where we had to go, not even at the restaurant were we ourselves again, and then in bed, when Joan stretched a hand towards me, I lay still, pretending to be asleep.

In the dark I could catch the uneasiness in her heart, could hear the bat of her eyelid, the unknown I was going to throw light on, the very next day, even if it meant turning her apartment upside down and consigning myself to hell in the process.

In the event, chance made the whole thing easy for me, because the daily cleaner phoned the next morning to say she had taken ill and so would not be coming for a couple of days, I could rummage at my ease then, without leaving any glaring traces of my search. The only thing I feared was that Joan might not go to the shop that morning, because of the mist that had risen at first light and now hid the trees from sight. I was also afraid she might stay in bed with me, and that the consequences of that act might cure me of any wish to probe her obscurer motives.

' 'Bye,' she said, putting on her fur-coat. She looked at me steadily as if she was about to confess something but in the end thought better of it.

'I don't know if I'll be back for lunch.'

'Just as you like, don't worry about me.'

'Well,' she said. 'Aren't you going to give me a kiss?'

I rose from the bed and went over to kiss her as you go to shut a window. I tried to preserve the coldness of manner I needed, and as soon as Joan went out, I slipped on a sweater, sat down at my work table, took pencil, paper, and the stack of picture postcards, and began noting the date, the place, the things about this journey or that one which I remembered as having some relation to Joan.

And at once I was struck by the feeling that Joan was dead to present life, was more like a woman loved in the past whose features, vices and virtues, I now strove to reconstruct. Even this autopsy was, as I was well aware, the highest act of love I had ever accomplished for a woman, going back over my doubts, the most equivocal incidents: a long galley of bewilderment and questionings that began with my return from Dakar at the end of June last year, but which could perhaps be dated from much earlier.

Anyway, this is where I had to start from, from

that first coincidence between my getting back early and her being away in Paris, she had said, and even allowing that to be true, what seemed most significant of all was her determination to go on behaving in a way that was already incorporated in some plan: 'Let's make a pact, that neither of us . . .'; but I had been the one to break it, to ask for explanations and detailed accounts from my partner, and meantime I had gone off to Gibraltar, and Joan had disappeared a second time, she had not set foot in the shop all day and there my flowers were waiting for her, then she had let the phone go on ringing, while I was with her, without answering, and only at Portovenere had she struck me as relaxed during those few days' holiday, up to the moment of her groundless alarm the afternoon I had lingered on the breakwater . . .

I got up, began walking from one room to the next, from the hall to the bathroom: from a hook her transparent shower-cap was hanging, and I suddenly found myself rolling this between my hands. Just as if it had been an investigation, I was setting in their order the pieces of evidence, the charges, the limits of the offence, and the cast-iron alibis. From the cap I picked out a long hair that had caught, I held it up to the light, Joan, I said to her, dear Joan, like a love letter, but then the same evening in the restaurant above Fiascherino, she had given in enough to confess: that they could hit at her through me, and, in fact, only when I was back from that little holiday, had I noticed Marcel's scars, and the way she herself avoided mentioning them.

*   *   *

I dissected, I dried out, I cut and sewed up, I explored her entrails, I mixed real skills and divination to drag a horoscope for the present out of the past. There was something else: two days at Marseilles, going by train to Nice and then by plane, or perhaps she never reached it, she had stopped off at Negresco where somebody was waiting or was to join her. A month of normal events, and then you come to the evening with Sergino when she had vanished from that eating-house on the Naviglio as soon as the police had arrived, and lastly the car on the motorway that had clung to ours all the way to Venice, Marcel coming out of her house carrying a mysterious little bag and Joan's explaining this immediately, even the maid she had had to get rid of, to leave herself freer, now there was a thread running through all this, and perhaps they were looking for no one but her, the evening the police burst into that eating-house, this is really fine, I said, I wanted an unusual fate, and so I had attached myself to a woman who knew how to vanish like the most expert criminal, if anything I could boast about it, and about her swimming too, her shooting, her driving so fearlessly, we were going through the Umbrian landscape like one of those great 'crib' settings, riding by little flat uplands and towers, shepherds in plaster and white heifers, from Spoleto to Orvieto to Perugia against the dark green of holm oaks, with their militia taking whole cities by storm, going through deserted picture galleries, we passed along the paintings in several panels, triptych, polyptych, what Joan calls comic-strips, inside and protruding from frames of the finest gold, and at the curve before you reach Todi—this comes back to me only now with the force of revelation—I realised we had a puncture, but she was the one to choose the best point on the road for changing the wheel, and as I was slow in inserting the lever, it ended with her doing it, not like that, first loosen the nuts, fine, and then wind the handle until it is raised clear, it seemed she had never done anything else in her life except get ready to take a man's role, to manage anything, to live rough, she who could indulge her every whim, and that was already pretty extraordinary, and from that time I should have begun to worry, asked myself what her perfection hid and what, her power of astounding me: just where do you get your ideas from, she had said to me, there's not a woman on this earth who hasn't asked herself what would it be like to act the whore, I mean, do it for money, but I had laughed at that, her brought up in luxury, who nonetheless had not the least fear of poverty, I had heard statements like that only in the villa of a Saint-Louis jeweller, built by the ocean, where dinner was cold caviare and champagne, those adventurers' faces ravaged by the colonial climate, and our hostess handed out bathing costumes to everyone so we could swim by moonlight, there were frogs leaping right into the courtyard, the storm was past, and as soon as we came out of the water, she and I went for a drive in her sports car, and on our return we could not see a living soul perhaps they were all in bed, each man with somebody else's wife, and perhaps among these there could have been Joan, I saw her, head lolling back over a bed, her bare shoulder bursting from the silvered dress, her shoulder which plainly bears the mark imprinted by teeth . . .

I threw open the wardrobe in her bedroom: the dress was hung there among the other evening ones, I had come to the bottom of my list, the inventory had been worked right through but I had not unearthed one other scrap of evidence, a new track suggested itself, and I stroked those silks, the sequins, the hair of the furs in a rustling of the different stuffs that hardly moved, wakened from the fixity of their embroideries, trimmings, the lifeless remains of Joan, impatient to show themselves entirely, and they crowd on one another, press together in an attempt to get free, the skirts that seem to keep her warmth in them, but no, inside the lining are mysterious folds, the belts made up so they can carry messages, medical supplies, ammunition or money, since the sending of important objects that are not bulky should be entrusted to women in whom the guerilla forces can trust entirely, seeing that women can carry these things from the village to the sierra using a thousand stratagems, buttons as dazzling as jacinth, the opulence of velvets, the listlessness of veils, the perfume released by them went to my head, the hand that strokes the hips, I hugged a dress at its waist and a sigh came from the breast of it with Joan's note, I squeezed those dangling arms, those diaphanous stuffs for the stage, golds, eastern fabrics, a flashing of scimitars, how far you have come to reach this, mistakes and pains, to reach a wonderful disaster, then suddenly I came right out of that fantasy, unloaded my booty, piled clothes and coats frenziedly on the bed, the capes and stoles, but their secret kept intact, and you ask yourself how is it possible to learn about her, a woman, when you have not learnt everything about yourself yet, and you have been dragging unanswered questions with you for too long now: questions about the obscure knots that make up your story, the frenzy of those Arabian sultans, and my mother's firmness in resisting for as long as she could, faithful to her Lombard precepts, stubbornly holding to her morality, to her limited notion of good, defeated ten times over by events as the snow-carts went by in procession on Corso Buenos Aires, a story you are now trying to read in Joan, you pass through the rooms again, searching for an action that desecrates, is decisive, the bathroom door was open, I went in, I opened the medicine cabinet, I drew out tins and bottles, pill-boxes, flasks, by the handful, feverishly I spelt out the names of innocent poisons, of extracts, of cures, there were droppers, little bits of apparatus in glass and rubber, this hygienic delirium as it ran its course was giving back her physical reality to me, I penetrated the intimacy of her body's fibres, instructions and methods of application that opened spy-holes on what I was looking for, I read endometriosis and hypo-plasia, each term suggested a trail to follow, there were gauzes and creams, these I could open and smell, and Joan had never been mine so surely as in this orgy of glass containers that testified to her weakness, the castanet rattle of the tubes I shook, tetracicline, stearic acids, chlorates, which succeeded one another like revelations, the limpid horror of the alcohol, a gale of spices, her odalisque step as she walks up out of a ship's hold, and it was really her, it was Joan who stood watching me from her doorway, awe-struck.

'But what goes on? don't you feel well?'

On the bed were piled her clothes, the wardrobe

door stood wide, medicines were scattered all about: not even a thief would have turned everything upside down like that.

'What about you? Weren't you staying out for lunch?'

'Certainly I was. But it's two o'clock now.'

'Oh,' I said.

'Haven't you had anything to eat? Or did you go out without shaving?'

Instinctively I put my hand up to my cheek, I was caught in a trap with no way out.

'When you want to rummage among my things, you might at least lock the outside door.'

She bent down to pick up a tube of analgetics that had rolled down on to the floor: I copied her action, and caught her hand.

'Joan,' I exclaimed.

Her eyes were as large and clear as ever.

We say stars light up just because by day we cannot make them out. Nevertheless it was only from a distance that I could measure Joan's brightness. I had tried exerting myself, had tried to work out some given facts of her behaviour quite rationally, but since between the diameter of the earth as it is at the equator and as it is, measured over the poles, you find, even allowing the sphere is perfect, a difference of fully twenty-seven miles, I had to draw the conclusion that I would go on loving Joan, without posing myself any more problems.

'In five days you've accomplished just about nothing, d'you know that?'

I did know, but now things were going a bit better. Perhaps it was a question of rhythm: I was not in the habit of sitting at a desk for hours, forcing myself to write like a professional, my attention wandered after a dozen lines, I was walking through Soho at night, or on one of the *quais* along the Seine, I saw the flashing red lights under the wing, ladies and gentlemen, fasten your belts, we are passing through a hurricane, I dozed against the plane's window, something had happened at Athens and into the telephone-kiosk came seeping the strong odour of *suvlaki* that a pedlar was roasting on the pavement.

'Promise me you'll work today, please—'

'All right, I'll try.'

I heard the door close. I was on my fifth day. I sat down at the table and began reading over the twenty or so pages I had already typed, only something was shining beside the curtain, on the floor, I saw it glittering against the skirting-board, I rose to pick it up. It was like a pen-nib, but much more pointed, of the same shape and size, that is, somewhat convex, but with a hole in the middle. I was still examining it under the lamp, turning it round intently, unable to guess where it had come from, when a flash struck me, a virus which grows active again just as the source seemed to be going dead and at once the infection is flooding, but of course, I said to myself, that was the first place I should have looked, where a firearm is usually kept.

I went to her bedroom, pulled out the drawer of her bedside table, sure I would find a revolver there. But no, only a comb, odd ear-rings, her cheque-book,

183

other papers that were of no interest to me either, all lying in confusion.

I was about to close it again when I noticed a picture, the corner of a photograph peeping from under a much-pressed tube of cream: it was a photograph of Joan in ski-ing clothes, from a few years previous, with her ironic, far-seeing smile, and looking more closely, I noticed there was a hand at her waist, a hand that could not belong to her as both hers were thrust into the pockets of her anorak, and, in fact, the photograph had been cut away on the side opposite to that hand, you could see the nicks the scissors had made, but I could not identify the place, a snowy slope with peaks like so many others, and there was no place-name on the back of it either, but that hand, cut off from its owner, became a presence that was all the more disquieting, a riddle to add to all the other unsolved particulars.

I went back to the seat at my work table, lit a cigarette. I had forgotten the tiny metal object, I was studying the picture now, I concentrated on the hand, certainly a male one, those fingers a little bit apart as they squeezed Joan's waist, and from her expression I tried to calculate the exact pressure, where the ribs end and there is that hollow which, when you press it, makes her start forward, graph curves from research on loving that, however, throw little enough light on the case, because there are ways of communicating, signs by which people can recognise one another, such as each having a half of a photograph cut in two, and moreover, at Amsterdam—I was remembering only now—Joan's car had been stolen right in front of her hotel, and who can say that it was true, she could have abandoned it herself, on purpose, from fear of reprisals, fear of an attempt on her life, organised in the night.

Groping my way, I was going on in pitch dark, and the malaise worsened with my powerlessness to define it in any reasonable terms, perhaps a fortune-teller, a seer, a magician would have read far more likely motives in appearances, I was thirsty, I got up to fill a glass with water: I do not know how, but it slipped out of my hand, exploded into a thousand fragments on the floor.

He is sitting in a circle with the others, his right leg, crossed over his left, has been seized with a nervous trembling, they have put out their cigarettes, closed the blinds, and are waiting for the lady to speak, the woman who has taken her glasses off and is dozing in the arm-chair with a rug over her knees, it is the first time he has taken part in this, some years after they had married and my father was secretly consulting those books, now his hand is cupped under his chin, there is a long silence, waiting for a miracle, uncomfortable, mock-Renaissance chairs, perhaps a lawyer's study, at the medium's back a shadowy book-case with doors of leaded glass, the smell of leather and brimming ash-trays, there, the first words dictated by the guiding spirit, mysterious greetings, a preamble in rhythmic phrases that comes from the beyond, up in the sky the buzzing of a Caproni hovering above the afternoon, and he watches how the unknowable acts itself out: sparks, particles, molecules chasing one another through space, mingling together in obedience to a law of love, of infinite, universal goodness, and we are nothing but moments of hydrogen stopped in time, atoms that are always becoming, helium and nitrogen, cosmic waves sped towards other worlds.

'From the haoma . . . to the weight-power . . .'

She is almost babbling, she clutches the rug to herself, the words can hardly come out: this necessary suffering as the way to knowledge, the ecstasy of perfection, and he listens in wrapt attention, finally eased in his earthly, everyday stalemate, by these truths that seem from heaven.

'You can ask questions,' someone said.

And he wanted to ask one, a question that is burning inside him, but he does not dare, being a new convert at his first seance, he has to hold his leg to stop it from trembling: if love may be enough to redeem us from a banal existence.

'Master,' they say to her. 'Master.'

And no one who sniggers at this Sunday charade, at the calm voice of the medium, beads of perspiration on her forehead.

'*L'amour c'est tout* . . . *L'amour: lumière, verité, la seule puissance* . . .'

Shade of Napoleon summoned up in this old property at Porta Vigentina, to compensate my father for so many futile hours spent at the office, but also to placate that sensual fury, to liberate him from the mould he was cast in, and planets and satellites made of pure Good spin through the dimness of the room, shining trails where before there were bodies and matter, fine dust of Spirit, and he listened, unmind-

ful of every carnal desire, overcome by the revelation
that he was vainly to try and pass on to me in after
years so that I might grow in the same faith as he.
Only today, faced with the powerlessness of reason,
was I recovering through him, in flashes, in floods
of light, the great allegories of the past, a design in
history, a personal system of the universe.

Then the lady fell silent, taken with a shivering fit,
huddled under the rug, a quiet rattling in her throat.
There was the sound of chairs being pushed back, it
had all lasted less than an hour, but now my father
knew he would never die.

'But oh yes!' I shouted. 'I shouldn't have done it and
I've done it all the same!'

'Please—don't raise your voice.'

Joan had not even taken her gloves off, she had not
had time: the moment she came in, she had noticed
the photograph lying right on top of my papers.

'It was mere chance, I certainly didn't want to
search through your drawers, but seeing we've come
to it, you can answer me now. Why have you cut
away part of this photograph? Who was standing
there, beside you?'

'And why should I answer you?'

'And why should I stay here in torment for days on
end, eaten out by questioning, tell me, why?'

There followed a pause, Joan was fighting down
her anger, she chose to speak out coldly, saying:

'Your bags are through there: you can go when
you like.'

'Is that all? You've nothing more to say?'

'I never told you to come and stay with me. You wanted to, you wanted to give it a try. All right: the try's a failure.'

'I asked for ten days.'

'Five have been enough. You see that yourself.'

She loosened her cape, sat down and lit a cigarette. In her gaze there was more hurt than resentment: of the sweetness, of the yielding mood that I had seemed to catch in the very first days, there was no trace now. I stood, a yard away, like someone in a middle-class comedy, fully aware of the string of stage-lines that I was about to repeat, because, after all, I had no choice but to act upon her suggestion.

I went into the bedroom, I brought out my cases, I began throwing in the shirts that I was taking from the drawers, and Joan came and leant on the doorpost, her lips moved as if she were about to say something to placate me, but I cut her short.

'I never spied on you, I never checked on your movements. And I could have done that a million times over.'

'By what right?'

I shrugged. We had been over this ground. 'I've a job, Joan, and unlike you I've a whole load of things I must attend to, and responsibilities, heavy ones. I can't go on, chasing after you like this. You see that?'

It seemed to me that I had wounded her, perhaps she was biting her lip, she was not even, when it came to it, so great a beauty, seen like this, on a typical winter morning, as I put away ties and shoes with a mounting fury that was aggravated directly by the packing itself.

'You're right,' she said abruptly. 'You're not made to live with a woman, at least with a woman like me. This is your destiny: to pack your bags.'

I was bent forward, thrusting my stuff well down, and I tried not to listen to her, exactly as I had done years earlier when I walked out of my own home, and it was this that humiliated me: this feeling of a second failure, and this time not my fault, while Joan went on, as if she were talking to herself.

'At least you might have seen that I'm a bit different from the women you've known. I could help you, you could do better work, devote yourself to the things that interest you, leave the paper, if it's true that you loathe it, but the truth is that you wallow in it, yes, in mediocrity, you, like all the others.'

Then I lifted my head to look her in the eye.

'Go on.'

'You haven't understood a thing: I could give up the shop, and the two of us settle in some other city, London or Paris, try living in a different way. I have had to become a warrioress, because that's what you wanted, but you, what have you become? Look at you: a little man running after his childhood, his pet dreams. Where's the man I knew, open-minded, full of courage and strength, you tell me, where has he ended up?'

A sob half stifled the last words. She put a hand up to her brow, to hide her eyelids which were perhaps wet with tears. The ash of her cigarette had fallen on her cloak, I could take a step and save myself with her. Nothing was done.

'You've dirtied yourself with ash,' I said.

Joan made no move, her face was contorted under

189

the pale make-up, but she did not answer, she still refused to account for herself.

The bags were packed, I put on my raincoat. I wanted to say : I don't think we have anything more to say to one another but it was pointless. I contented myself with a brusque farewell.

'Cheerio,' I said, pushing my bags towards the lift.
'Goodbye,' murmured Joan.

The bad actions of others put our mediocrity in a favourable light making it look meritorious. My decision gained on the score of pride the moment I compared it with her conduct. In fact, it struck me as no unworthy way to put an end to a relationship that had lasted too long. I was back in my room, like a monk's after that flat of Joan's, but above all a melancholy place, as rooms little lived in become. I found a heap of back mail, urgent letters with cheques in them which I had even forgotten to call for, I had been so taken up with thoughts of Joan in those five days.

We had never really walked out on one another after a quarrel. In the past we had tried to separate several times but always by mutual agreement, first coming to a joint decision, or one of her proposing, that it would be wiser to finish things.

I had to do something at once, apart from hanging up my clothes again and all the rest of it, something to stop me thinking and suddenly I realised that I no longer had friends, only colleagues at work, passing acquaintances, and this, too, proceeded from her: that I should have chosen her for friend and confidante, she was even educated to man's talk. I could have resumed work, saved what was left of my holiday for a better occasion, but I did not feel like it. Perhaps the best thing was to let myself be in peace and freedom: go to a concert, read books, take walks.

Solitude turns us to lofty undertakings. But these always subside when we begin to see people again. So I went out to dine alone in an eating-house I used to go to, in the vicinity of Sant'Ambrogio, then I looked for a bench where I could sit out in the open, in the square. A pallid sun was beginning to break through the greyness. I breathed in space: the near-by basilica, the robust courtyard with its pillars, the balcony with the dwindling arches, I had no need to see any of that, the power in those structures so close at hand strengthened me, I would bring my daughter here one of these mornings, I would tell her the tale of the Carlovingian kings who are buried there, Anasperto's severity, but then I had only to take my eyes off an object and I felt the wound burning again, the emptiness led me back to Joan, I did not want to ponder her last words now, I would have plenty of time later, I was no longer soothed by the thought that a disaster could decide things for us, the sight of her face disfigured in the crash: I knew by myself that work, any work, without a woman is less than nothing.

Two interminable days had passed. I had set myself

to work at the book again, with grim determination. It was one more way of communicating with her. I was perfectly aware of that, and also of trying to show her how wrong she had been about me. There were moments when, in myself, I harangued her, I made the same accusations all over again, or I cleared myself of blame, I thought up attenuating circumstances and at the end I was left wondering if our story had really been concluded, with no chance of appeal.

So my hopes were dashed the moment after the phone rang.

'I don't understand,' I said. 'Who is it?'

'*C'est moi, Yvette.*'

She had stopped off at Milan the night before, but had not managed to trace me, however as her next plane was not leaving till that evening at least we could meet over a meal, always supposing that I . . .

'But of course, Yvette.'

After all, she would distract me, I called at the airport to pick her up: she was in great form, brown with the sun of Rio, where she had been the week previous. I took her to a restaurant in the centre of town, instinctively choosing the streets and places where Joan or one of her friends might run into me.

'And so, you didn't get married?'

Luckily: she explained that the fine young man had shown how terribly jealous he could be in time, and that was something she could not bear, no woman should, she asked me did I agree with her, but of course, I said, finish your ice-cream, and then we'll go up to my place to talk at our ease.

'To talk?' Yvette, with a meaning smile.

And yet no sooner was she there than I regretted it.

It could have been a sort of holiday, after all, a pleasant interlude, but I could not shake off my anxiety, as if, from one moment to the next, Joan might arrive, I gazed at her long legs as she squatted on my bed, they were more perfect than Joan's, but they expressed nothing, like a doll's limbs, even right up at the thighs.

'You look as if you've never seen me before.'

'It's not that, Yvette, I was thinking.'

'About what?'

I began lying again as I had almost always done with all my women, believing in it myself as long as the embraces lasted, and the shuddering and the sighs, of the kind a man of forty has in his repertory. If I thought of what I had looked for in Yvette, I had to persuade myself that, over and above her body, her resistance had seduced me, her petulance, her easy sureness and the whim of the thing, the eagle with outspread wings embroidered on her jacket over the right breast. But now I could not deceive even myself. I broke away from her like some one impotent.

'What's wrong? Don't you like me any more?'

'It's not that, it's me. I'm sorry.'

It seemed bad taste to tell her about Joan: Yvette loosed half out of her clothes and already offered. I offered her a drink of whisky, but I could not find a clean glass. She had got up, began to pull on her things, staring at me reproachfully, she refused to stop another minute. As it was, I would never see her again.

How she is now, with her arm bent back on the head-rest of her chair, so little removed from my lips, how many days come between us, darling, murmuring, naturally, things that are so common, the springtime of blood, the muscles it hides, only she and I know what it means, thank God something of ours was left out of all the words printed and broadcast, and she is gazing ahead, as if posing, with her straight, her incorruptible profile, and she does not speak even here, in this picture gallery where you have come looking for her, passing by, to get out of the traffic, from the Saturday bustle, when I had let myself be infected with the same fever as the rest, when, newly married, we took the big stores by storm, up and down the escalators, signing cheques like declarations of war.

Now I had gone back to eating with people's chatter for company, snatching a bite, my pockets loaded with telephone discs, the typists on the stools in the snack-bars, black smocks showing under their over-coats, and coffees ordered loudly, as if they were proclaiming a personal privilege. I went right back, forced down to the bed-rock of my story, to the first days after I had left my wife, the squalor of those rooming places, the telephone with a lock on the dial, and a telephone directory hung in the lavatory as toilet paper, the feeling of winning a short-lived free-dom, and that anyway the battle was somewhere else, and all the same it would be good to have done with it, deliver oneself over for ever, and the beetles coming out of my father's shoes, the black and white ones kept in the little cupboard under the wash-stand, were the same beetles that the electric light flashed to sight on the plaster of those walls, the heaters all but dead because the landlady used to soak the coal so that it would last longer in the boiler, and the nights spent shuddering with cold, with a laughable hint of greatness in them, urinating in the wash-bowl so as not to have to go all the length of the corridor, what did Joan know about all that, she who could not bear the smell of people in a lift?

Without noticing it, I had come all the way to the district where we used to live. From a good way off I saw the façade, I counted the floors, the balcony where my daughter took her first steps, I was coming back from a bout of love-making, this had happened several times, a trite escapade, purely sensual, to let me feel I was still alive, and they were watching from the balcony; their faces radiant with smiles, merry no matter what, deepened my sense of guilt, but also the decision to have done with hypocrisy and the daily lies, you haven't touched me for two weeks, she had said coming up to the balcony rail where I stood in thought, and then the parcel at the foot of the Christmas tree, the collection for the flood victims, there are so few things that make us indignant now, and rain falls on us without wetting, protected as we are by good central heating, preparing for a sleep that is better than a cordial, on the contrary, it is perhaps just here that we recover our composure: in the silent tumbling of the washing-machine that fades in the model-girl's smile, this is where we reckon what our day has come to, at peace with our wounds, and we wanted to launch a revolution.

So you go down the steps into the underground, get into a carriage like a robot, carried along by the tide you come up into the air again, it does not matter in what part of the city, and you will not even admit that what you are seeking is a fine gesture, certainly this is not your city any longer, but a metropolis only half-awake, in spite of the notice that invites every-one to the meeting to be held on Friday evening at nine, the notice is shining with wet, the paper swollen, almost spongy, there is something fleshy in its big type, or perhaps it is the speaker's name that a crack in the wall has split in two, those crumbling letters that you feel like scoring there with your nails.

'How are you getting on? Don't you recognise me?'

At least you should remember those eyes, that look of fire.

'Of course,' I say. 'Aldina!'

Luckily she does the talking, about the two young boys she has by the hand, the older holds the umbrella up, about herself, this with real emphasis, about her home, then about me, about the progress I have made in my career, about my articles which she sometimes reads.

'Yes, I'm married too. I have a daughter.'

Just for an instant as she held out her hand in fare-well, she seemed disturbed beneath that wife-and-mother make-up. On another occasion, who knows, we would have been perfectly frank with one another.

'Pardon the glove.'

You stood stockstill, watching her go off under the rain, feeling proud, notwithstanding everything, that she was still Aldina with the lovely legs (the tears you made her shed for nothing), and you carry on along the tree-lined avenue, taken by your own steps towards the gateway of Porta Romana.

196

I had never done it before: I crossed the wide square and went up close to study the great oak doors, a good hundred years old, the stone medallions set into the thick wall of the gateway which saw Napoleon march through, I read those names, the little photographs of the men who fell to the bullets of the Nazi-fascists, the fallen of the Porta Romana section of the Resistance, images that were tragic in the winter rain, mocked by the sun in summer, along-side the great gate thrust wide open to the Motorway of the Sun, and we drive forward when the light is green, heedless of these tiny oval portraits, with their good Milanese names, Consonni and Fontana and Galimberti, honour won in other times, to be read with the Latin inscriptions, along with the soldiers of the Grappa front who had a baker's shop in Via Orti or a coal yard in Corso Vigentina, useless dead of yesterday, and I said to her: Joan, what has all this been for?

Two days later, I had two more left before my holiday ended, I was really working at the book at last, and they phoned from the paper: I had to come back now, not later, and be ready to go off on a job.

'You're all mad,' I answered. 'Leave me alone.'

They put me through to the editor.

'What d'you mean?' he said. 'Haven't you been reading the papers?'

That was the truth: for days now I had forgotten about the rest of the world. Nonetheless, something big was under way in the Middle East and it could become interesting.

'Interesting?'

'Yes,' he replied. 'Both sides have mobilised. Better take a look.'

So call-up papers had come for me too. The next morning I would be at the airport, to disembark at Tel Aviv and sleep God knows where. I had little time left. The day before I had taken my daughter to the circus, I had held her hand right through the performance, speaking to her as I would have spoken to Joan, amid the whipcracks, the lions, the daring leaps, then catching my breath with her as the drums rolled for the twists and turns another Joan did on the trapeze, airy and unreachable as never before, while she swings above our heads followed by the beam of light, shining in her silver tights, her body swaying from the bar, the muscles tensed as she springs, the statued groin that belongs to her alone, and then why not admit it, that this is the only certainty left you, and in this you still try to escape (every other hope in the struggle gone) from the agony of being dead, and you hold to the body of a woman, Joan, with the frenzy of a boy, and you tell yourself, something will happen, further on, as worthwhile as this.

I was afraid that if I were to call straight at the shop, at her place, I would not find her there, perhaps the shop itself had changed hands, what lady, the girl-assistant was saying, please wait, I don't understand, but everything was untouched, Marcel was busying himself in the backshop, I call him, he turns round, I tell him, strip, and he obeys, he has taken his shirt off, and on his back and shoulders he has not

198

even one of those scars any more, it was I who imagined them, one more hallucination, no harm in it, and they were speaking to me slowly, smiling with great sweetness, until I decided and composed Joan's number.

There was no answer. I called the shop, her voice made my heart jump.

'It's me,' I said. 'I must see you. I am off tomorrow on a job.'

'Oh,' was her reply, and it could have meant anything, disappointment or indifference.

'I'll call and pick you up in ten minutes.'

'No, I was just going out on an errand. Wait for me at four.'

'Where?' I said.

'In Piazza della Vetra.'

Even the condemned man himself breathes again, once his appeal for a reprieve has gone in. But later, seated on a bench in the square, the doubt that she may not come, the anxiety as you wait for sentence, for her regal stride out from the porch of the old Tax Office, at four sharp, these begin to quiver, throb, and you begin to lose blood in the sunshine of a mild February when even the dead are waking in the cemetery's blades of grass, the sun puts strange colour on the bricks of San Lorenzo, and children chase one another behind the church's east end, and a ball is bouncing on the earth of this square notorious for all time.

Now you know what it is about: about all the curses

we carry inside us, one of them will bring us low in the end. It does not matter on what day : what matters is that every cell that goes to make up your fury finds its bed in these stones, this light, in the mists, in the worn gravel that three hundred years of sunsets and rain have washed from the blood of that day in August.

It was four o'clock and still Joan did not come. I waited for her to show proud in her white lace cuffs, the pearl necklaces joined together on her bosom, through the crowd I glimpsed the light of tragedy thrown momentarily by the whited skins, the fine strands, the spittle dribbled on the black of the velvets, signs of illness, messengers of violent death, the waving shape of the halberds, the iron of the pikes, the fine steel of the blades, and I was at the Three Kings Inn, a pitcher of wine before me, watching from a distance the crowd as it gathered, the elegance and the blood, the blade of a sash, its hilt of lace, the executioner's nails.

It was past four o'clock and still Joan did not come: then the man, *adhibita ligatura canabis*, gave a half turn, the cord went taught, and there was, as it were, a shuddering of bones drowned by a moan, and his limbs stretched to the agony, it being the year of Our Lord one thousand six hundred and thirty, because here Joan should show, that she might find you with the others, *impinctos de aspersione facta Mediolani unguenti pestiferi*, with the same desperation upon you, as you begin to taste the tugs on the cord that keep time with turns of the screw, and suddenly the cloudiness blotted out the sun, the grass was stained with bile, the walls with flesh, a sea of heads thronged the square, red with the heat, and that whiff of death coming from Carrobbio, and another throng on the doorsteps, barefoot, their kerchiefs knotted over their brows, at the window-sills of the farther-off houses, arms raised threateningly above heads, howling with the terror that seized on all of us on the morning of the 22nd April when the walls of many houses were found to be smeared, the marks scattered, irregular in size, of yellowish or dark saffron colour, as if someone had daubed the walls with a sponge: the terror of other houses smeared since that day and of people infected as soon as they touched them, doors, chains, or corners, and even the benches in the cathedral having to be burnt; the terror that in the churches moved them to empty the water from the font, as some persons, unfearing in their wickedness, had dared to go about smearing the very house of God, and similarly the grind-stones of mills, like the seven men from Volpedo tortured on the wheel; nor did a man live in fear of his neighbour and friend only, but fear came between father and son, between wife and husband, and the bed that is held to be sacred excited terror.

Because of this, the square is now thick with people, this muster of citizens that to you brings back the barber shop situated in the said district, on the corner looking towards the Carrobbio, and his anguish, the said barber, forty-five years old, burly, with a white and red face, his beard and hair inclining to fairness, meanwhile upon the cart, with white-hot pincers, *candenti forcipe vellicetur*, they fasten on his flesh as he is led to the place of execution, and it is your cigarette end burning your fingers in the by now hopeless wait for Joan, because the diabolical spell is of such a kind that he who is taken by it has such relish and delight in going about smearing, that no other pleasure may equal it.

I looked at my watch, and a dull roar rose from the mob, the cart had appeared escorted by the executioner's men, and the two wretches upon it, blood dripping from their arm stumps because their right hands have been cut clean off on the very spot where they manufactured the hellish smearing mixture: wind raised the dust on the square, softened the outline of the stake fixed in the ground and the wheel resting at its foot, mercy, I murmured, cursing the resistance that stood up to torture, the guts forced into the throat, and again the inquisitor's voice composing out loud: 'The man interrogated says: this smearing mixture was made of human excrement and the spittle of plague victims, and I delivered it in exchange for a hundred ducats' and again on the 26th of June so that he may tell the exact places that he smeared: 'he answers: in the Carrobbio district', anyway it is all over now, we shall give in to raving madness, from the instant the executioner strikes once more on the bar of the winch, and the howl covers the creaking of the shoulder bone wrenched from its socket, we shall confess what they want if they will only stop this agony, of Joan who will not come, now that you can make out the dregs of Milan hanging from the trees in the square to enjoy the last act, after they have broken the bones as is the custom, *frantis ei de more ossibus*, and following the sentence, he is to be twined on the wheel, still living, and after six hours of being exposed as a public example, is to be strangled at the executioner's hands, in the delirium of the shouts, the laughter and the insults of the snouts pressed on window sills, the plumed caps at the high windows, until from the threshold of one of these openings broke, incredibly, her perfect figure, she came over the gravel towards me, to the bench in a heavy booming, as the bell struck the quarter hour.

'Joan,' I rose up to take her hands, to make sure they were hers. 'How are you?'

Now with her beside me on the bench, I spoke to her as I would to an invalid, not finding any other way to declare to her that she is air and light and everything I have missed for days now.

'How d'you expect me to be?'

I kissed the palm of her hand in gratitude.

'Three centuries ago, at that point just in front of us, they executed Gian Giacomo Mora, one of the smearers, you know, at the time of the plague.'

'And you've come here to tell me this?'

On the circuit where the Naviglio canals once ran, the cars went roaring by, one after another, the boys were shouting in the middle of the grass, at a stroke everything turned inexpressible again.

'Joan, all these days . . .'

I was looking down at the ground, and my gaze took in her silken limbs, I thought of the first time they were ever revealed to me above the skirt line, of her arms, the colour of her skin.

'All these days I have been thinking of you, of us.'
'Well?'

'Nothing: I've got to leave town tomorrow. They called me up from the paper; perhaps I'll be away a week, perhaps two, I don't know yet.'

At last we looked at one another; in her eyes there was no desperation. As always she, and she alone, was ready for anything, even if it meant not meeting again.

'I was afraid you had left town yourself. Or that you wouldn't come just now.'

'I've never done that.'

'I know you've never done it, Joan. Perhaps it is because you've accustomed me to things like this: to living in uncertainty, to knowing so little about you that I'm always afraid of losing you, that I'm forced to imagine things about you like a man possessed.'

She listened to me, calm and ungraspable, knowing only too well what answers to give, ones I could read, unaided, in her look: how love is nothing else but this uncertainty, torment, madness. She did not say that, against my egoism, against my ruthlessness (if ever I could come to the point of being tired of her), she had nothing to set but this way of surrounding herself with little secrets, of secluding herself, escaping me, inventing a second life so that I would go on chasing her and loving her as I did at first when I waited for her at Silver's behind the curtains, my heart thumping at every trill of a phone, my whole body trembling at a footfall on the stair, chasing her through showers and latrines, undergrounds and alleys, low attics, escalator mazes, along iron hand-rails, tiles and mirrors and neon lights, the hell under and outside heaven.

'Joan, I understand now: never get tired of making me run. It's enough if you stay with me.'

She slipped her sun-glasses on, perhaps I had shaken her but she did not want to show it, a cold wind had risen and the sun was going down within the dark lenses.

'You know it's not easy for me either, loving you, making you run, being the warrioress you want. I'd like to stop and rest, myself, be an ordinary woman, let myself love simply as any other woman would.'

She spoke, and there was that wonderful feeling you have when you arrive by train early in the morning, at a great city, the same spectacle of natural might, vitality, of cars in the outer suburbs, waiting in columns at the traffic lights, to converge on the centre, all together running towards something unknown that is there in the middle, in the city's heart, in a new day of bicycles and clanging trams and lorries and factory smoke rising in the foul air, everyone getting up with the hope, never fulfilled, that today will be different. She spoke, and there was the bitterness there at living in a world where no one grows indignant any longer, with the lucid awareness that truth is outraged, principles mocked, that everything is born already corrupt, condemned to meanness, and that only the single act counts, the faith in a lost resistance, these for their own sakes.

'You wanted risk, uncertainty, love that is proved day by day. But then once you really had that, you asked for guarantees. You wanted to know, you tried to break the pact.'

She spoke, Joan, and you have never been more aware of how blind we are to the existence of another enemy (even as we prepare for a frontal assault), the real enemy to be defeated who lurks in our own selves and who, only a little earlier, had been undermining you, like an illness, right in the midst of the struggle, and once more you are ready to gamble everything for what you lack, for a love.

'I want you, Joan. I'll learn, you'll see. I won't make a song about it, not again. Please darling.'

Slowly and in silence the crowd emptied from the square. High on the wheel, hoisted to the top of the pole, stayed the tortured man, breathing his last. I, too, had reached the end of my agony.

' 'lo, princess.'

I stroked her hand once, Joan sat beside me on the bench but regally, almost without touching the thing. We entrusted our last words to our fingers. Our hands met, they twined together gently, then suddenly gripped one another tight.

'What time do you leave?'

I shall tell her later, when we are back home and have repeated acts that we know, our breathing no longer a panting, in that fulness she gives you every time, I shall tell her that we could make it so that I do not have to go at all, and, if she helps you, try living, as she said, in a different way, on the near side, and on the far side, too, of defeat.

'Come,' Joan said.

We got up, moved off together. And the dusk was gathering, just as it does at the end of those novels that Joan detests, and you could hear, clearly, the first, far-off rattle of the shooting.

(3018)

£ 3200 -

023001

A/70